SO-AFY-540

RUTH LANGLAND HOLBERG

Mrs. Holberg was born and educated in Milwaukee, Wisconsin. She attended Milwaukee Art School, hoping to illustrate books for children. Instead she married Richard A. Holberg, already an established and famous artist, who illustrated the books she wrote until his death in 1942. Since then other artists have illustrated them.

Mrs. Holberg lives in Rockport, Massachusetts, a picturesque old New England town on the Atlantic Ocean. Of it she writes, "This is a fine place for a writer of children's books to live. There is much opportunity to observe children and there are many interesting ones to know. The setting offers much for the stories because Rockport has many historical legends and fascinating old houses."

The author is a renowned cook and writer of several very successful cook books as well as stories for boys and girls.

The
GIRL IN THE
WITCH HOUSE

The GIRL IN THE WITCH HOUSE

by Ruth Langland Holberg

Illustrated by Lloyd Coe

HASTINGS HOUSE · PUBLISHERS

New York

Copyright © 1966 by Ruth Langland Holberg

All rights reserved. No part of this book
may be reproduced without
written permission of the publisher.

Published simultaneously in Canada
by Saunders of Toronto, Ltd. Toronto 2B.

Library of Congress Catalog Card Number: AC 66–10518
Printed in the United States of America

JF
H7239

For *Moira*
Sean
Leslie
Kim
John
Jed
Gregory
Kirsten

84417

The
GIRL IN THE
WITCH HOUSE

• CHAPTER ONE •

*D*AME Higgins taught school in her own house. Wearing a shawl over her plain gray dress and a ruffled white cap on her head, she eyed her restless pupils on their long wooden benches as they read from a primer. The class had only one book because primers were rare.

"Jennifer Rowe," she snapped. "Stand up and read where Carrie Babson left off."

Jennifer felt Carrie nudge her sharply with the primer. She had been staring out the window at Carrie's old dog Rusty as he made his way to a spot under the gooseberry bushes. She thought he was acting queer. He flopped down on the ground with his feet straight out and his head back.

As Jennifer read from the page where Carrie had finished, she heard Carrie giggle.

"Be seated," Dame Higgins scolded. "If you don't pay attention, you will have to sit with the beginners."

Carrie's snicker made Jennifer turn red with anger. Carrie teased her often, saying she was stupid and homely. Jennifer knew she was plain but she did not think she was any more stupid than the other eleven-year-old pupils.

Somehow the slow morning passed. At last the time came for eating her lunch of cold cornbread and she sat quietly by herself as her schoolmates teased each other. The boys yanked Carrie's red-gold curls and offered her chunks of gingerbread but no one offered Jennifer anything, and no boy pulled her long brown hair hanging over her shoulders.

After lunch Dame Higgins rang her handbell to call the pupils to order. "Stop your noise and get your slates ready for a writing lesson."

Jennifer tried to keep her mind on her work but she did not do very well. Her slate pencil scratched out capital letters in straggling rows. At last Dame Higgins told the children to stand for singing. Jennifer smiled and stood up, eager to sing. She had a sweet voice and enjoyed singing at home the songs Grandpa Rowe had learned as a boy in England. The family sang them together when they were working in the fields or sitting around the fireplace in the evening.

Jennifer heard Carrie singing out of tune and frowned at her. Carrie in turn stuck out her tongue at Jennifer.

"She doesn't like me." Jennifer said to herself. "I guess nobody in school likes me because . . ." At that moment Dame Higgins clanged her bell. "School is dismissed," she said.

The pupils rose and dashed into the yard. Carrie Babson stood in the doorway calling her dog, "Rusty, Rusty."

Jennifer's thoughts flashed back to Rusty lying down under the gooseberry bushes. She ran to look at him and her eyes filled with tears because she knew Rusty would never come running to Carrie again. She walked up to Carrie. "Rusty is dead," she whispered. "He is lying under the gooseberry bushes."

Carrie turned and cried, "He isn't, he isn't!" But her brothers ran to the bushes. They came back slowly and the youngest whimpered. "Rusty won't wake up."

Carrie flew to Rusty. She looked and looked at the quiet old dog who did not wag his tail or open his mild brown eyes when she stooped to pat him. She wept and called his name but she knew that he did not hear her.

Then she turned to Jennifer. "You are glad Rusty is dead. I hate you. You never liked Rusty."

Jennifer's heart hurt as she heard Carrie's sobs but she admitted, "I didn't like Rusty when he bit my sister Mary, who was trying to rescue a cat from him."

"Rusty never bit anyone!" Carrie shrieked.

The other pupils stood around watching the quarrel. Carrie cried, "Your sister Mary is a witch. You live in the Witch House and Rusty knew Mary was a witch, so there."

Dame Higgins came out. She took one look at the dog and said, "Hush this racket. He died of old age and I'll have him buried down yonder in the back pasture. Now you all go home. Carrie you must learn to control that bad temper of yours."

As Jennifer slowly turned to leave the yard, screeches followed her. "Your sister is a witch and you live in the Witch House."

All the way home Jennifer thought of the reasons why her house was called the Witch House. In the beginning the house had only one large room and a tiny bedroom. It had been built by two sons for their mother. They had fled with her from Salem to Cape Ann way back in 1692, because the mother had been accused of being a witch. She would have been hanged on Gallows Hill if they had not left.

As the years passed new rooms had been built on until it became a good-sized house. Some people thought it was cursed but Jennifer's father did not believe that and was glad he could buy it cheaply because of the story about the witch. Mr. Rowe was a cooper who made barrels for fishermen to store salt fish in. He knew there was plenty of work for him in Pigeon Cove and in Sandy Bay, a busy fishing village nearby.

Mrs. Rowe was happy to move into a large house even if it kept her very busy. Mary, her first daughter, had been a sickly child and could not be of much help. Besides, Mary was an odd girl. She had dreams and visions of things about to happen. The neighbors said she too was a witch and some people thought that being born in the Witch House was the reason Mary was queer. But Jennifer had been born in the Witch House, too, and there was nothing strange about her. She was a practical girl, and a help to her mother, but she was troubled by the teasing of her schoolmates about the house. "Your sister is a witch, Jennifer Rowe, and we don't want to play with you. You live in a Witch House."

So Jennifer kept apart from them and hurried to get away from their taunts. She kicked the dust in the road as she slowly came close to the Witch House. She thought about the great fireplace in the keeping room. It was a comfortable room but she did not know if it had been blessed as was the custom in the early days of building. The two sons were supposed to have placed a treasure between the stones in the corner of the fireplace, but she was not sure about it.

Jennifer sighed. "I guess our fireplace was not blessed. I guess Mary is a witch because she knows things others do not know. Maybe the house *does* have a curse on it." Her mood grew blacker and blacker.

"Nobody in school likes me because Mary is queer and the house is queer, too." She turned off the main road and walked through a grove of trees. The rising wind shook the trees and the sky grew dark. A storm was brewing. Jennifer looked up when she came into the yard and saw Grandpa waiting for her.

"Jennie, your face is tear-stained. What happened?" he asked.

She flung herself into his arms. She told him the sad story of Rusty and how Carrie had said Mary was a witch.

"Now, now." Grandpa smoothed her long hair with loving pats. "Child, Mary is not a witch. But first let me tell you how much Mary looks like my sister in England. She, too, had a way of knowing things before they happened. So did my mother, who came from Scotland, and the people there called it second-sight. They thought it quite natural. Many people have hunches and dream about things that are going to happen. No one calls them witches. I know it is hard for you to understand this."

"But Granpa, Mary was born in the Witch House. Doesn't that make her a witch?"

"Jennie, Jennie, so were you and Cyrus," he said.

She began to cry. "But he is a boy and only girls are witches."

Grandpa gave her a little shake. "Stop your nonsense. Here comes your big brother William. Give him a smile."

Jennifer watched William come toward them from the barn. She loved him dearly and they were very companionable. "What shall I do when . . ." She stopped. The secret she shared with tall lanky William would soon be known to all the family. William took one look at her woebegone face and hugged her.

He teased, "I'm starved, sister. Why aren't you helping Mother get supper?"

She flew from William and Grandpa into the house, determined to be cheerful and do all the chores her mother expected her to do. Suppertime was close and there were many duties Jennifer always tended to.

CHAPTER TWO

JENNIFER filled the pewter bowls with hot cornmeal mush from the large kettle hanging in the fireplace. Her mother brought a wooden bowl of apples and walnuts from the dresser and placed it in the center of the long trestle table.

"Come and sit," she said.

Expectant faces smiled at the steaming mush. Each person sat on his ladder-back chair or on a stool, except for Cyrus, the youngest Rowe. He stood at his place and as soon as his father glanced at him he recited grace.

> *"Here a little child I stand*
> *Heaving up my either hand,*
> *Cold as paddocks though they be,*
> *Here I lift them up to Thee,*
> *For a Benison to fall*
> *On our meat and on us all."*

A murmured "Amen" followed the grace. It was hardly heard as the storm howled down the chimney.

Cyrus pulled his stool up to the table and sat down to eat with good appetite. There was a jug of molasses and pitcher of milk to pour over the mush. For a few minutes all were quiet as they ate.

Then Grandpa Rowe spoke, "I remember paddocks in our garden back in England. We thought they were lucky."

Jennifer held her spoon suspended. "Grandpa, you told me they were toads. No one calls them paddocks here in Pigeon Cove."

Jennifer's older sister Mary said in her dreamy voice, "I rather like 'paddocks'; it sounds nicer than 'toads,' which I think is an ugly word."

No more was said about paddocks or toads, for the early spring storm grew louder and the rain splashed down the broad chimney into the fire below. The coals hissed and the boisterous wind puffed the fine ashes over the pine floor. Jennifer's father had an anxious look as he turned to his brother Thomas.

"Tom, it is a bad night for you to go off through the woods to Gloucester. Can't you wait a day or two?"

Thomas said firmly, "I tell you that I must go at once. Yesterday a man came into my shop and told me that twenty boats were out in the fishing grounds, a short distance from shore when news came that the British were marching on to Concord." He had told the story before to the family but that did not lessen the shock. Thomas went on. "One boat went off and notified the others and they all returned to shore. We will be armed tonight and ready to march to meet the enemy."

Jennifer watched William when her father suggested that Thomas wait until the storm was over. His face was troubled. He was going to run away from home to join the Gloucester forces at dawn. He was going to follow his Uncle Thomas, who did not know of William's plan. Thomas had his own mind so set on getting into the war to free the American Colonies from British rule that he had no room for other thoughts.

Many times Jennifer had heard her father talk about the injustice of the Tea Tax. Two years ago, in 1773, chests of tea from England had been taken from three ships at Griffin's wharf in Boston and dumped into the harbor. Her father had said, "I think it was the only thing to do that December day. By the great horn spoon, if I'd been there, I'd have dressed up like an Indian too, and I'd have been one of those sixty men boarding the vessels and I'd have hurled one of those three hundred and forty chests of tea into the harbor!"

Grandpa sighed deeply. Jennifer could see that he was torn between his belief that the English king could do no wrong and his steadily growing love for the young colonies.

Grandpa was a Tory, but he was beginning to wonder if he was right in his views. He had been brought up in England and he loved the English king. It was very hard for him to accept Thomas's feeling for the American Colonies. He could not accept his eldest son Josiah's feeling either. Josiah was Jennifer's father. Grandpa could not understand why the colonists wanted to be free from English rule. He had left England when he was a young man and his sons had never known, as he did, how deeply the royal family was loved and respected.

Grandpa said, "I remember how that tea was worth nearly a hundred thousand dollars and now the British have closed the port of Boston to punish the colonists." Then he cried out, "It isn't fair! I never thought the king would be so unfair."

Jennifer's mother watched her family with sorrow. She was a quiet woman who wanted only peace with her loved ones clustered about her.

Jennifer hated to think how sad her mother would be when she discovered that young William had run away.

The storm grew louder with rain pelting the sturdy walls of the house. Cyrus yawned and snuggled up to Jennifer. "Will the British come here and shoot us?" he asked her.

"No, Cyrus, they are way off in Boston and they would never find Pigeon Cove or the Witch House. You're sleepy and I'll take you up to bed."

Cyrus kissed his father and mother and went with Jennifer up the steep stairs to his trundle bed. When Jennifer tucked him in, he whispered, "Sing to me, Jennie."

Jennie bent over his bed. Her long brown hair fell forward and she brushed it into place behind her ears. She wished she had a red ribbon to tie it back. She sang,

> *"Hush my dear, lie still and slumber;*
> *Holy angels guard thy bed,*
> *Heavenly blessings without number,*
> *Gently falling on thy head."*

Cyrus relaxed and snuggled deeper into his bed. Jennifer tiptoed down the stairs. The family had left the long table and were sitting around the fire. She picked up the bowls and spoons and washed them. Apple cores and scraps were set aside for the chickens and ducks.

Uncle Thomas watched her slender but sturdy figure move rapidly and quietly around putting things in order. William gave her a loving pat and a curious aching look as she passed him to brush the nutshells into the fire with a big turkey wing used for that purpose.

Jennifer loved William and it was hard to keep his secret. She did not let herself think how sad she and the others would be in the morning when they discovered that William had gone to be a soldier.

Jennifer sat down next to Mary, who moved over on the settle, and the sisters smiled at each other. Mary's blue eyes grew misty and took on a faraway look. The young men who knew Mary or even caught a glimpse of her fair sweet face and flaxen hair, fell in love with her in spite of her reputation as a witch. Jennifer laughed at them. She understood Mary and she knew that not one of them had a chance. Last summer, Jennifer had sat with Mary under a tree in their grove, listening to the gulls crying inland.

"It makes me sure that there is going to be a storm," Mary had said.

Jennifer felt herself stirred by Mary's words. The sea was just half a mile away and it raged up the rocks with a mighty surging strength.

She leaned against Mary. It was a very warm day but she shivered, and suddenly was half afraid. She whispered, "What is it, Mary? What do you see?"

Mary murmured. "I can almost see him, the man I am going to marry."

Jennifer laughed and said, "Come Mary, stop dreaming. We must pick strawberries for supper."

Mary was silent for a moment and then she said again, "I can almost see a man lying on the flat rocks down at Haulabout Point."

Then the spell was broken, for little Cyrus came tumbling through the long tangled grass calling, "Mother wants the berries right away."

Jennifer jumped up and tossed back her long hair. "You help me, Cyrus." She caught his hand.

Mary lifted the wooden bowl to fill with strawberries and together they went to the garden back of the big barn.

Jennifer's thoughts of that summer day were interrupted by the announcement that it was bedtime. She and Mary went up to the bedroom they shared.

The storm was dying out now, leaving broken branches in the yard. There would be plenty of work the next day.

• CHAPTER THREE •

*T*HE family had all gone to bed. Uncle Thomas rolled up in a blanket and slept on the floor in front of the fireplace so he would not waken anyone when he left at dawn. A final gust of wind blew a branch from one of the elms, throwing it against the house. The crash roused Jennifer. She crept from bed, being careful not to wake Mary, and looked out the window. She could not see much, it was so dark, but she thought she could make out a figure tugging a broken branch from the path that led to the well. It was Uncle Thomas, she was sure. William was going to follow him later.

The figure disappeared. She knelt at the window for a few moments and then crawled back in bed. She was restless thinking about William tramping through the wet woods, but sleep came to her at last.

Breakfast time was always busy. Her father built up the fire.

"Where is William?" he grumbled. "He should be bringing in dry logs from the woodshed. Will, get up, you sleepy-head."

There was no answer. Jennifer watched her father go to get dry logs. Her mother was stirring cornmeal mush and poking fat pork sausages that sputtered in an iron spider.

Jennifer wondered what William would be having for breakfast in Gloucester. By this time perhaps the forces were marching to Boston.

Her father came in with the logs and laid them on the hearth.

"Jennifer, bring in fresh water from the well, like a good girl." He smiled at her quick obedience, then went to the narrow stairway and shouted. "William, get up at once or I'll take a stick to you!"

She hurried to the well. Her father had never whipped his children. He was just out of patience. When she had drawn up a bucket of water with the windlass, she came back slowly, knowing that William's disappearance must have been discovered.

She found her mother in tears and her father looking as if he had been stunned by a blow on his head.

"I can't believe it," he muttered. "Will is too young to be a soldier. He should have told me and not left this scrap of a note."

Jennifer knew, as had William, that his father would never have allowed him to enlist. Grandpa Rowe came in from the back bedroom where he slept. He listened silently. Then he spoke up. "William's got fighting blood in him from way back. Stop pitying the lad, would you have us crawl like cowards?"

There was complete silence. Jennifer stared at Grandpa Rowe. She asked, "What made you change your feeling for the British king?"

Grandpa Rowe grinned. "We ought to be glad for William's determination to fight for the colonies. I have been doing a lot of thinking and it makes me boil with anger everytime I think about unjust taxation." He paused a moment and then added, "Don't forget the lad is with his Uncle Thomas."

Grandpa Rowe went to Jennifer's mother. "Come now, Abigail, your son is almost a grown man and gone to be a soldier. Be proud of him." He patted her on the shoulder.

Somehow the family gathered around the table. Somehow, in spite of aching hearts, they ate the good hot food put before them.

Jennifer finished quickly and then went upstairs to wake Cyrus. She was torn between two feelings. One was the sadness of having William run away. It was natural that Uncle Thomas should go to fight the British but it was not easy to have a sixteen-year-old brother go gladly into danger.

The other feeling concerned Grandpa Rowe. Up until this morning the family had been ashamed and embarrassed with their stubborn old Tory. Neighbors had gossiped about his loyalty to the hated English king. Some had even planned to tar and feather him and ride him on a rail through the village. Jennifer knew how worried her father had been. Now that dreaded threat had been removed.

She woke Cyrus and helped him put on his shirt and breeches. She smoothed his hair and washed his hands and face. Cyrus said, "I can do that myself. I'm a big boy and I want to go barefoot. I hate shoes."

Jennifer dried his rosy cheeks. "It isn't warm enough yet to go barefoot; you'll have to wait till summer. Besides you are lucky to have these good shoes that Uncle Thomas made. Who will make shoes for us now, I wonder?"

Cyrus was ready to go downstairs for his breakfast. When he finished he joined Jennifer, Mary and Grandpa picking up fallen branches in the yard.

Jennifer was helping Mary lug a heavy branch away from the front door of the Witch House when she looked around for Cyrus. He was not in sight. She dropped her end of the clumsy branch and ran down the path to the main road. There was Cyrus, begging a fisherman to allow him to blow the horn that called housewives to the road.

As Jennifer reached the horse and wagon, Cyrus put the horn to his lips. Out came a penetrating blast and several women hustled from houses scattered along the main road.

Jennifer took Cyrus by the hand and bobbed a polite good morning to the fisherman. He grinned. "I got a fine haddock today."

Jennifer said, "I think my mother will need one."

"I see her coming." The fisherman blinked at the figure hurrying down the path between the elms. "Mighty wild storm last night. I see you lost some limbs from those big trees, Mistress Rowe."

By this time half a dozen housewives gathered at the fish wagon. They glanced at Mrs. Rowe's face, stained with tears and saw her trembling mouth. Sympathy and questions brought out the news that William had run away to be a soldier. Some of the women knew how she felt, for other boys in Pigeon Cove had done the same thing.

Jennifer watched one woman who was famous for her sharp tongue.

"Humph," she grumbled. "How about Grandpa Rowe? Miserable old Tory. He's probably mad and raving to have William stand up for freedom from the British."

Jennifer took a deep breath. "No, Ma'am. Grandpa is glad that William isn't a lily-livered coward. He says William will do us proud. Grandpa says he is all for fighting the British rascals!"

For once Jennifer sputtered with temper. She was usually a quiet little girl and the neighbors were shocked to hear such talk. They exchanged glances. Of course a girl whose sister was a witch would be queer! It was generally known that Mary had knowledge of things before anyone else did.

The fisherman snickered. "Good for Grandpa Rowe. He has finally seen the light. I'll spread word that we no longer have a Tory amongst us. Now there'll be no tar and feather party." Then he slapped a fine haddock on the scales which Jennifer's mother bought for dinner. Jennifer could see how straight her mother stood now, her lips turned up in a firm smile. Whatever had brought about Grandpa's change of heart, it had taken her mother's mind off William.

Cyrus tugged at her hand. "Come and race with me, Jennie," he begged.

Jennifer laughed. Her heart was lighter and she teased. "See if you can catch me, Cy." She tore ahead and the two of them came to a breathless stop at the side door. Jennifer said, "You beat me; you win, Cy."

"Stay out and play with me, Jennie," the boy pleaded.

She shook her head. "I have to polish the table and put the potatoes on to boil. You go and help Mary." Jennifer gave him a little push.

"O Jennie, she isn't any fun," Cyrus pouted.

Jennifer went in to do her work. Grandpa was resting and smoking his pipe. She gave him an impish glance from her brown eyes.

"Did you change your mind suddenly?" she asked.

"No," he chuckled. "I have been mulling over this question of loyalty but I kept it to myself until today. Then it seemed the proper time to speak up, to ease the loss of William. We should stick together as a family."

Jennifer began rubbing the table to a glowing polish. Often she sang as she worked, but today she went about her tasks quietly, and with a sober face. There was just too much to think about.

· CHAPTER FOUR ·

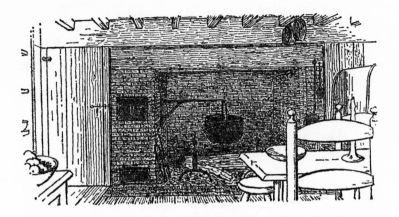

S*ATURDAY* morning the family was too busy to mourn William's absence. Jennifer heated the oven with sticks of maple until its walls were very hot. Then she scraped out the embers, making a clean place for the bread and beans to bake.

Mrs. Rowe mixed rye and cornmeal for bread. She put the loaves to rise in a warm place. Later she tucked them into the oven to bake. The hinged iron door was closed and not opened for hours.

There was a small sandy beach about half a mile from the house where clams could be dug. Mrs. Rowe sent Jennifer, Mary and Cyrus to dig some. Trotting along the road with buckets and clam forks, they chattered about the pigeons flying in great numbers above their heads.

Cyrus said, "I want a pigeon pie."

Mary said, "Why don't you wish for steamed clams? Wish that we get a peck of clams."

"I hate steamed clams. I hate . . ." He looked around for something else to add to his list of hates. "I hate . . ."

"Cyrus, be quiet," Jennifer demanded. "Here come some children."

She watched three little boys and a girl approach. They were the Babsons walking toward Sandy Bay.

"Hi, Carrie," Jennifer said.

Mary murmured, "Hi."

The three boys teased Mary. "Witch," they yelled.

The smallest boy asked his sister, "Why is she a witch?"

Carrie said spitefully, "She was born in the Witch House."

Then the Babsons ran along, stopping only to pick up a few pebbles to fling at the Rowes.

Cyrus yelled, "I hate you. I hate you!"

"Hush," said Jennifer. "It is wrong to hate people. I don't hate Carrie. I wish Carrie liked me."

She looked at Mary, whose usual calm expression was changed to one of sorrow. Mary said, "It is sad to have people think our house is cursed. Father says it can't be cursed, because it was built by two loving sons who brought their mother from Salem to Cape Ann."

"Do you think if the sons had placed a treasure in the chimney the house would be a blessed one?" Jennifer asked.

Mary smiled at Jennifer. "You are the only one in the family who has that notion. Plenty of houses are built without treasures placed in the cornerstone and they are not cursed. I have always felt that our house was a good place to live in."

Cyrus lost interest in the subject. He ran ahead crying, "I want to go wading."

Jennifer and Mary hurried along. Jennifer saw Mary lift her face to the tender blue sky that stretched over the budding trees. It was April. The gulls were far out following a fishing boat, looking for the entrails of the fish being cleaned on board the vessel.

The Rowes reached the beach. The tide was low and

they took off their shoes and stockings and trotted down to the damp sand with their clamming forks and buckets. Cyrus waded. It was a peaceful hour with no hint of war or danger.

Going home they were overtaken by a team of oxen pulling a low-wheeled cart loaded with granite. It stopped when the young driver walking beside the oxen approached the Rowes.

"Hi," he called cheerfully. "Want a ride?"

Cyrus broke away from the girls and shouted, "I want a ride."

The young man's smile when he saw Mary was wonderful to behold. Jennifer said to herself, "That is the way they all look at Mary, as if they couldn't believe their eyes. She is so lovely and fair . . ."

Jennifer was eager to hop on the wagon. Mary, with a quiet air, gave the driver a smile and she too stepped on the low cart.

"Been clamming?" the driver asked.

Jennifer nodded yes, as they rumbled over the rough road. It was not easy to keep their balance.

"Where are you taking the stones?" she asked.

The driver said, "To Sandy Bay. They are going to build a church with a stone foundation."

Jennifer's eyes were bright with interest. "Oh, then we can go there to church. Did you hear that, Mary?"

Mary loved the church in Annisquam, but it was a long walk through the woods, over Gingerbread Hill to Lobster Cove where the old church stood.

Jennifer saw that Mary was not going to be drawn into any conversation with the driver. Jennifer thought he was a handsome young man, but good looks meant nothing to Mary, nor did flattery or devotion have any effect on her.

"I don't think any boy will ever ask me to take a walk or go to a dance or skate on a moonlight night. I'm too plain." Jennifer thought to herself, "Just a little brown bird like Mother . . . a brown bird singing. That is what Father calls her."

She remembered hearing how they had met at a singing society when her father was a tall sturdy blond fellow with a golden tenor voice. She could hardly picture him like that for now he had a limp because a log had fallen on his foot and the bone had never knitted properly.

Jennifer's thoughts were interrupted by Mary, who said, "Here we are, wake up, Jennie, we must get off."

The driver slowed the oxen and the clammers hopped off and called their thanks. They trooped into the house with their clams and helped to clean sand from them. Saturday duties went on as usual and evening arrived with tub baths for everybody in turn in front of the fireplace.

There would be no church going the next morning for the wood paths would have to be cleared of branches that had fallen during the week.

The following Sunday morning Grandpa decided not to go to church. He was not much of a church goer, anyway. The simplicity of the Annisquam church did not appeal to him for he had grown up in the church of England. He liked its more elaborate ceremonies with all their kneeling and chanting.

"Keeps a man from falling asleep," he often said. "I like the smell of incense, too."

Cyrus had sniffles so the family was glad to have Grandpa there to watch over the restless boy. "I'll tell him stories about when I was growing up," Grandpa said. Grandpa always had time for the lively boy's questions and his strong arms were a ready refuge for Cyrus.

Jennifer and Mary walked behind their parents through the wooded path. It was exciting, Jennifer thought, to see the silver pussy willows bursting from their sticky brown envelopes.

"Mary, see the fern fiddleheads. We should come here

to gather some this week while they are young and tender."
Jennifer pointed.

Her father and mother stopped on the path and Mr.
Rowe picked a posy of blue and white violets, giving them
to his wife.

"Abigail, carry them. They become you," he said.

She flashed him a smile of pleasure. They walked on
their way with birds singing cheerfully and it seemed as if
nothing could mar the peace of this April morning.

The church stood at the head of Lobster Cove. Its
doors were open to drive out the cold that loitered in every
corner of the building and to let in the soft April air. The
sexton tolled the bell. Friends greeted each other soberly
and went to their seats in the square boxed pews.

The parson took his place. He turned an hour glass up
to measure each hour.

When the final blessing was pronounced they rose
gratefully from the hard seats to go into the noon sunshine.
A rider on horseback came galloping from the direction of
Gloucester. He waved his three-cornered hat and yelled,
"Wait . . . I have news!"

The congregation stood together, fearing the worst.
There was something terrifying in the man's face as he
rode nearer to them.

"At Lexington . . . and Concord . . ." He gasped
for breath. "On April 19, the militia forced the British to
withdraw!"

The people clustered around him, waiting for his next
words.

"Eighty-eight of our forces were killed, more were
wounded." His voice was hoarse with emotion. "The British lost two hundred and seventy-three lives."

Tears filled Jennifer's eyes and she clung to her father's arm. He looked down at her with loving eyes. "Come
my small brown bird, let us go home."

The family was very sober. Jennifer helped her

mother. They came to the table and were served warmed-over beans and dried apple sauce sweetened with wild honey. Jennifer offered Cyrus some gingerbread but he was so miserable with his stuffy nose and cough that he ate hardly any.

When they rose from the table, Mr. Rowe said, "Now that the first blood has been spilled, we must be ready for the hardships of war."

"Why, Father?" Jennifer asked.

Mr. Rowe explained. "With the British ships on the ocean and in Boston harbor, our ships with supplies may not be able to get through."

Jennifer's mother shook her head. "Grandpa, our garden must be bigger so we can raise plenty of food."

Grandpa leaned over to pat Cyrus on the head. "I have a good helper here and the girls will tend to the chickens and ducks."

Mr. Rowe smiled at his family. Then his face grew serious. "This skirmish may be the beginning of a revolution," he said.

· CHAPTER FIVE ·

M ONDAY morning Jennifer went off to school. One of the oldest children there, she would soon finish with Dame Higgins. After that came a school taught by a man in Sandy Bay. Many children never went to school after they were twelve, and Jennifer hoped she would not be sent to Sandy Bay.

Figuring was especially hard work. When Dame Higgins tried to make her understand the abacus, Jennifer felt very stupid.

The abacus was a wooden frame with wires strung from side to side. Colored beads slid back and forth on the wires. She could count the beads, but when it came to subtraction and addition she had trouble. Dame Higgins pushed the beads too fast, she thought.

She tried hard that morning but it was not easy to keep her mind on school work, knowing that each passing hour might bring William into danger now that the war had begun.

At lunch when the pupils gathered to eat and chatter,

Carrie Babson was always the center of interest. Jennifer and all the other girls envied her handsome dresses and her large hazel eyes and reddish curls. The curls were always tied back with a green or red ribbon.

Carrie's gleeful voice burst out. "I'm invited to a dance at the Rogers' house!"

All the girls stared with unbelieving eyes. They had never known anyone of their age to be invited to a dance at the famous big house the Rogers owned in Gloucester.

"I'm going to wear a silk dress and new slippers," Carrie said.

Jennifer burst out impulsively. "A silk dress! What color, Carrie?"

Carrie drew herself up proudly. She held her nose in the air.

"Pooh, what do you know about silk dresses, Jennifer Rowe, the Witch House girl?"

The others giggled and snickered. Jennifer wanted to get up and slap Carrie. She knew what a silk dress was because her mother had her wedding dress, which was being saved for Mary's wedding when Mary finally decided on some young man for a husband.

Dame Higgins came in then and called her pupils to order. The lessons went on and on. They recited the multiplication tables together and took turns reading from the primer. At last the bell rang and school was over for the day.

Jennifer did not linger to talk with the other children. She hurried home where her mother was making soft soap and needed her help.

She flew to the backyard. "Mother," she called, "I'm home. And I'll stir the soap for you."

Taking the wooden paddle from her mother, she began to stir the mess in the big kettle that hung over a brisk fire. She was careful to stir in the same direction her mother had been stirring, for luck.

For months all the grease and wood ashes from the fireplace had been thrown into a barrel with layers of straw between. A little water was poured in now and then and it dripped through the ashes out a seep hole at the bottom of the barrel. This was called lye, and every bit of it was saved.

Straw kept the coarse part of the ashes from clogging the hole. It made a horrible smell when the grease and lye were boiled together.

Jennifer wrinkled up her nose. Probably her clothes would smell of grease and lye for days. At school the children whose clothes smelled of grease were seated by themselves at the back of the room.

After an hour of stirring she grew weary. Mary came to take her turn and Jennifer went into the house. "How is the soap now?" her mother asked.

Jennifer sat on a stool near the fireplace. She was thinking about Carrie's silk dress.

"Jennie, didn't you hear?" Her mother's voice was sharp.

Jennifer looked up. Her mother seemed to sag with weariness. "Mary thinks it will soon be time to stir in the salt," Jennifer said.

Mrs. Rowe took a wooden bucket of salt and Jennifer followed to watch as she added salt to the soft soap to make it harden. It was then poured into wooden frames to be cut into bars when cold. It was a harsh soap that cleaned the washing but reddened and roughened the hands. Mary used cucumber juice on her hands and face to keep the skin soft and clear.

The fire under the kettle burned down. The soap was poured into the frames and the iron kettle stored in the barn. Grandpa came to feed the chickens and ducks. Cyrus was begging to be allowed to feed the ducks. He was cranky and feverish from his cold. Before anyone noticed, he wandered over to the duck pond and climbed into a flat homemade boat moored to a willow tree.

He pushed off after untying the rope and stood up with a single oar. "I'm going far away!" he shouted.

Nobody heard him. Jennifer and Grandpa were hunting eggs in the manger of a stall.

A group of cows came ambling into the barn to be milked. Jennifer watched, thinking it was time she learned to milk now that William had gone to be a soldier.

She heard Mary screaming, "Grandpa, Grandpa, come quick!"

There was a note of shrill terror in her voice. They ran out to see Mary at a little distance, standing at the edge of the pond.

Mary pointed and Jennifer saw the boat in the middle of the pond. "Cyrus is under the boat—I saw him fall out of it! Hurry, Jennie!" Mary's voice rose in a scream of anguish.

Grandpa had taught Jennifer to swim. She plunged into the pond and swam to the boat. She held her breath and ducked down. Her hands touched Cyrus and she pulled and yanked at him, trying to hold onto the side of the boat at the same time. She found she could stand up on the muddy bottom of the pond and just keep her nose above water. With all her strength she held Cyrus until Grandpa waded in to help her.

Cyrus was rushed to the house and Jennifer stepped out on dry land, dripping wet and shaking from the ordeal. She sat on a tree stump and took deep breaths until her pounding heart grew quiet. Her glance rested on the old house. It looked to her like a friendly house with its unpainted clapboards weathered almost to silver. The windows were like eyes looking out to welcome people to come live there.

But Jennifer was too wet to sit thinking and she hurried into the house where her dress dripped on the floor and her shoes squished.

Her mother exclaimed, "Jennie, you poor child, go

into Grandpa's room and take off every stitch. Here is a warm blanket to wrap around you."

Jennifer shed her wet clinging clothes and wrapped the blanket around and over her head and body so that when she came out bare-footed, there was only a plain little face peering out of the blanket. She sat beside Cyrus and Mary gave them both a hot toddy.

The unaccustomed spirits in it warmed her quickly and soon she was cosy and dry and ready to put on clean clothes.

Mr. Rowe came in and heard all about Jennifer's rescue of Cyrus. He hugged both children and they went to eat their supper with a prayer of thanksgiving.

Evening came and the blueness of the sky melted away into lemon and rose and soon it grew dark. A few early stars pricked through the dusk. Jennifer knelt at the bedroom window sill, wishing on the first star, wishing she might have friends. Then she said her prayers and climbed into bed beside Mary, who was already sleeping quietly. Jennifer felt sweet and clean and tired and a moment later she, too, was sound asleep.

• CHAPTER SIX •

S *CHOOL* was over. One day Dame Higgins declared it closed because the boys were needed for farm work and carpentering; others whose fathers were fishermen, had to dig clams or dry fish on the racks. Jennifer was kept busy at home or assisting her father. She was doing some of the chores that had been William's.

"Jennie," her father said, "I want you to go with me to Hoop Pole Cove. I'm going to cut wood for barrel hoops."

Jennie smiled. This sounded like fun. She loved the low-lying swampy ground where wild cherry and birches grew.

They started out early one morning, walking along the shore and then across flat granite boulders. Jennifer's father was quiet and she thought how good it was to be with him.

Once they came to the swamp, Mr. Rowe cut slim branches and Jennifer piled them into bundles. They moved among the trees all morning. By noon they had worked their way into the rough open headlands. They sat on boulders in the sun to eat their lunch.

Jennifer's thoughts went back to Carrie's silk dress and new slippers.

"Father," her voice broke the silence. "Do you know Carrie Babson's father?"

Mr. Rowe looked surprised. "Yes, I know him. A good man and his farm over yonder is neat and prosperous."

Jennifer looked earnestly at her father. "Is he rich?"

"Why, Jennie, what is the reason for all this interest in the Babsons?" Her father smiled at her upturned face.

"Well," Jennifer began, "Carrie is going to a fine dance in Gloucester at the Rogers' house and you know that is the biggest house in Gloucester. It even has a ballroom, so Carrie said. She is going to wear a new silk dress and have new slippers made just for the dance and she will wear a velvet ribbon in her hair. She has curls, too."

Mr. Rowe reached out to hold up a tress of Jennifer's tangled locks. "This hair is as brown as a bird's wing and as lovely." He comforted her.

Jennifer beamed. Then she was serious again. "If I should be invited to a dancing party, I wouldn't have any slippers. Uncle Thomas could have made some, but now he has gone to be a soldier and I don't know the new cobbler. He would have to be paid, too."

"Jennie, you are too young to be thinking about slippers for dancing." Her father stood up and held out a hand to her. "Come, let us pick up the bundles and go home."

The slender branches were light but awkward to carry. Jennifer's slipped off her shoulders and while she stooped to gather them together she sniffed the air. "Look, here is a big patch of catnip!"

Her father helped her balance the bundle on her back. "You must gather some when it has grown taller and before it is discovered by others. Catnip tea is good for folks' ailments."

"William told me that people buy it for their cats. He knew a printer's boy who made lots of money selling it from house to house in Sandy Bay and Gloucester," Jennifer said.

They started homeward and the bundles were finally piled in the cooper's shop where Mr. Rowe began to peel them. Jennifer went home.

She was about to open the side door when she heard the sound of horse's hoofs. She turned to look down the winding lane between the elms and saw a rider waving a piece of paper. He drew up his horse and looked down at her. "I have a letter for John Rowe," he told her.

A letter was a rare event and she murmured, "That is my grandpa, sir."

She ducked a curtsy and opened the door. "Grandpa, she called. "Come here, please."

To the rider she said in a shy voice, "Will you come in, sir?"

In no time the dusty rider had dismounted and walked into the Witch House. Grandpa, Mother, Mary and Jennifer stood with anxious eyes and tight faces, dreading bad news.

Grandpa broke the seal on the folded letter. He said, "It is from Thomas. He is fine and William has been promoted because he can shoot so well. That's because I taught him hunting in these woods," Grandpa bragged.

He read on. "Now listen to this." He turned to them. "We are training in Ipswich and expect to join the forces in Boston any day now. They say the Redcoats are handsome young men and I don't see how I can fire at them."

Jennifer wanted to cry with sorrow for the young Redcoats. She hoped William would never have to shoot a man, Redcoat or not.

Then Grandpa read more of Thomas's letter. "Our men enlist very slow and our Enemy has got a reinforcement of five Regiments. If the New Army is not raised in season, I hope I and all my townsmen shall have virtue enough to stay all winter as Volunteers before we will leave

the line without men, for our all is at stake. If we do not
exert ourself in this glorious Cause, our all is gone and we
made slaves forever, but I pray God that it never may be
so."

Silence followed the reading of Thomas's words. Jennifer did not understand it all. The man who brought the
letter was invited to sit down and have some refreshments.
He and Grandpa talked between themselves and Jennifer
ran down to the cooper's shop to get her father. Mr. Rowe
hurried home and joined the men drinking mugs of
switchel, a mixture of molasses and cider, cold water and a
pinch of ginger.

Grandpa returned to the first part of his son's letter. "I
am in need of shirts and breeches. I am afraid I shall wear
you out with my sending you so much work but I cannot
get anything done here so I must beg your patience."

Grandpa looked at Jennifer's mother and Mary.
"There is work for you two. Have you linen to sew into
shirts and wool for breeches?"

They nodded, yes.

The bearer of the letter rose from the settle. He
waited long enough for Mary to write an answer and fold
and seal the letter. All that Grandpa had to say to Thomas
was to ask for more news of William. He promised they
would send him two shirts and a pair of woolen breeches
as soon as possible.

The rider left and Cyrus stood waving his goodbye.
He had stayed outdoors admiring the horse and feeding
him grass.

"I want a horse," Cyrus declared.

"You've got a hobby horse," Jennifer reminded him,
but Cyrus grumbled. "That is only a stick of wood with a
wooden horse-head on top. I want a real horse that smells
horsey with a long mane and tail and I'll ride him far away
even to Sandy Bay."

Jennifer laughed at Cyrus. He was fun. She said,

"How would you like to take a walk with me to the quarry? I want to see if any berry bushes are in bloom."

He grinned and took her hand. They trudged over a rough path that led to the quarry and beyond it to a stony expanse of ground covered with stunted trees and juniper bushes. Here, in the summer, were to be found blueberries, huckleberries and blackberries. Swamps nearby had dense thickets of hemlock, white pine and white oak.

Cyrus ran shouting toward the swampy ground. "Come back, it's too dangerous to go into the swamps," Jennifer called. "Help me look for bushes that show signs of berries, especially elderberries."

"Why?" Cyrus asked.

"You like them stewed with cranberries and honey. Mother makes wine with them, too."

Cyrus said, "I want to go home."

Jennifer remembered her father's words about raising enough food to carry them through war time. It looked as if there would be a large crop of berries if the summer was not too dry.

She raced Cyrus home and then helped Grandpa feed the hens and ducks and bring in fresh water from the well. Her mother had a fish chowder bubbling gently on a trivet near the blazing pine logs.

The twilights were growing longer and after supper there was time for Mr. Rowe to go off to the cooper's shop for an hour or more of work. Grandpa spaded a flower garden. He had already dug a vegetable garden and hired a man to plow the cornfield. Jennifer and Mary planned the flower beds, calling back and forth now and then to Mrs. Rowe, who had seated herself on a wooden bench built around the biggest elm tree. It was still light enough for Jennifer to see how tired her mother looked, as she bent over her sewing in the fading light.

"Mary, is mother feeling poorly?" Jennifer whispered.

Mary nodded her head, yes, and whispered back. "But

she will feel better soon, you wait and see. It's nothing seri-
out, so don't worry."

The answer did not satisfy Jennifer but Mary shook
her head as a warning when Jennifer started to question
her further.

After an hour or more, Mrs. Rowe folded her sewing
and called, "Come girls, it's bedtime. One of you go and
tell Grandpa that Cyrus must come in."

Jennifer found Grandpa and Cyrus in the barn. Cyrus
was explaining to Grandpa, "My horse is going to have this
stall and I will name him Rover."

Grandpa laughed and chuckled. "My boy, that's a
dog's name."

For a moment Cyrus thought hard. Then he said
firmly, "My horse's name will be Rover because I like that
name."

Jennifer interrupted. "It is bedtime, Cy, come with
me."

He took her hand and chattered on about his horse.

By this time the sky had grown dark. When Jennie
looked up she saw little stars sparkling with sharp points, as
if they were very young and curious stars peering down to
take a look at the Witch House.

CHAPTER SEVEN

THIS was the time of the year when the peddler was expected any day. He carried packs of fascinating goods in his wagon besides tin cups and dippers and milk pans that hung around the sides. He was a welcome visitor at the Rowe house and Jennifer was eager to see what he would have to show them.

"Come in," Mrs. Rowe invited. "Let me see your calicoes and needles."

The peddler said, "That I will, ma'am. Thank you, ma'am."

They watched him with interest as he opened a bundle. It was full of buttons, combs, fragrant soap and many other articles. Jennifer's mother selected the things she needed for sewing. She bought a length of fine white muslin that seemed too delicate for ordinary use and Jennifer wondered what it was for. Her gaze was fastened on rolls of velvet ribbons, green and red and black and gold. She saw Mary pick up a string of blue beads and look at them as if she would give anything to own them.

Grandpa and Cyrus waited for the other bundle to be opened. Cyrus made a dive for a bright red horn. "Grandpa, buy it for me!" he begged, and hugged his grandfather until Grandpa handed it to him. "Now, you go outdoors and blow it," he ordered.

Cyrus dashed out, blowing, "Toot-toot, toot-toot."

Jennifer's mother was interested in the bright-colored rolls of calico. There was a tantalizing smell from the sizing in the goods that mixed with the spicy whiffs of ginger and cinnamon and green coffee beans. Coffee was a rare and expensive drink. Jennifer heard her mother remark, "We can't afford coffee until it gets cheaper and of course we don't have tea any more, what with the heavy tax the British have put on it."

The family spent an hour gloating over the store of goods displayed by the peddler. Mary was delighted to have her mother buy the blue beads for her. Jennifer had her choice of flowered calico for a dress. When all the purchases had been made and the peddler had mended some pots and pans with his tinsmith's tools, he was invited to stay for dinner.

Afterward Mary went to sit on the bench around the elm tree with her sewing while Jennifer helped her mother. They watched the peddler tie up his bundles and as he finished he said, "Your sister isn't as much help as you are, Jennie."

Mrs. Rowe laughed. "Mary is a dreamer and her head is in the clouds most of the time."

The peddler smiled at Jennifer standing in the doorway. Her mother said, "Jennie doesn't dream, she is right down to earth."

The pedler's deep-set eyes bored right into Jennifer's heart as he said, "Jennie has her dreams and wishes, too."

This thrilled Jennie and she said to herself, "He really knows me as I am." Then he did a surprising thing. He opened a bundle and took out a roll of red velvet ribbon and cut off a length just right to tie back her hair. She was speechless when he gave it to her.

"You will need this ribbon for a very special and unexpected pleasure. Keep it for that day."

She managed to thank him and then the peddler drove off toward Sandy Bay with his horse and wagon and its treasures and its rattling of tin pans.

Jennifer ran to sit beside Mary on the bench. "See what the peddler gave me, Mary!" She held out the soft velvet ribbon, as red as the heart of a ruby.

"Dear me," Mary exclaimed. "Where will you wear such a lovely thing? Certainly it is much too gay for church and it does not go well with your plain brown dress."

Jennifer's voice was warm with pleasure. "He told me there would be a time when I would wear it, a happy time."

Mary was silent. Then she spoke as if from some deep dream.

"Yes, the day is coming when you will wear the ribbon and I shall wear my blue beads and the man I love will be beside me. We will find him lying on the flat rocks and he will be wearing a uniform . . . I am waiting for him. . . ." Her voice drifted off. "I feel as though someone was telling me . . ."

Jennifer shivered a little. Mary's words had a way of coming true—but this dream was too spooky to be true.

"Jennie, Jennie!" Mrs. Rowe's voice rang out.

"I'm coming, Mother." It was time to prepare supper and Jennifer worked steadily as she sang the song she loved.

"Lavender's blue, dilly, dilly,
Lavender's green, dilly, dilly."

Before long her mother's voice joined hers. Grandpa came in with a bucket of warm milk and he beamed. "I like to hear singing." He blended in with his rumbling bass voice.

The next morning Jennifer woke early at the noise of a window opening. She sat up and peered through half-opened eyes at Mary leaning out over the window sill.

"Mary," she whispered. "What are you looking at?"

"There was no answer. Jennifer climbed out of bed and went to the window. It was just before dawn. "I dreamed . . ." Mary spoke in a far-away voice. "I dreamed I found him on the rocks. I must go to him."

"It's too early." Jennifer yawned, but Mary began dressing. Jennifer did not want Mary to go alone and thought to herself, "I'll go with her and I can look at the catnip along the way. If it is tall enough I can pick some of it and peddle it from house to house. Then when I have lots of money I will ask the cobbler to make me a pair of dancing slippers."

By this time she and Mary were dressed. They left the bedroom on tiptoe so the stairs would not squeak or creak. Jennifer continued her thoughts. "Red slippers, I think, would be best with my red ribbon."

As they slipped down the path between the elms and oaks, birds were stirring in their nests with little sleepy twitters that became full-throated songs by the time the girls reached the main road.

The sun lifted itself above the horizon and the sky was flushed with pink. Jennifer felt as if she had wings on her feet. She ran and skipped and searched for catnip.

Mary stood gazing over the quiet waters. Then she turned away and Jennifer, stopping to watch her, followed her.

"The time has not come, but it is coming. Let's go home," Mary said.

"Oh, wait a minute," Jennifer cried. She dashed to a patch of catnip and knelt down to examine the husky coarse stems and young leaves. But they were not yet big enough to pick. She broke off a sprig and hurried after Mary. On the way home they met a cat trotting out of the

woods. Jennifer called, "Kitty, kitty." The cat was shy and
eyed her with suspicion. But she held out the sprig of catnip and watched the cat's eyes open wide. Its face lifted up
and in an instant a pair of impatient paws took the catnip
from her fingers. She laughed to see the cat rolling in the
catnip and rubbing its cheeks against the leaves.

"Cats like catnip and I will gather lots of it so I will
have enough money for dancing slippers." She hurried
along with Mary and when they turned into the Witch
House path, she hummed. "Red slippers, soft and pretty,
for dancing."

No one noticed the girls' absence. Mary went to their
room while Jennifer brought up fresh water from the well.
Before long she had breakfast ready.

"Today," her mother announced, "I am going to dye
some lengths of woolen cloth for Uncle Thomas's
breeches."

"What color?" Jennifer asked.

Her mother said, "I have some clusters of dried stag-
horn sumac, which will dye the wool a pale tan color."

She went on, "Jen, you help Grandpa with the big
kettle. He is building a fire out where we made soft soap,
you know. Fill the kettle half full of water and when it
comes to a boil put in this cloth bundle of dyestuff. Let me
know when you do that."

The morning was spent with many errands back and
forth. At last the tan woolen material was dyed and hung
on a line to drip and dry.

After dinner Jennifer saw Mary slip into the grove of
elms and oaks. The sun poured through young leaves and
spread golden circles at her feet.

Jennifer felt drawn to Mary's side. Mary spoke to her.
"I must go now to the rocks. Come with me, Jennie."

Jennifer was moved by Mary's emotion and strange-
ness. The two girls walked to the flat granite boulders
around Haulabout Point. Usually there would be a few

gulls cracking clam shells or scolding each other with eerie cries.

Today not a gull was to be seen or heard, but Mary spied something else. She scrambled over the rocks and slipped into pools of tide water, while Jennifer followed, crying, "Be careful, Mary, you'll break an ankle, be careful!"

At the water's edge, she saw Mary reach the body of a man in uniform. Kneeling beside him, she touched his face and pressed back his wet dark hair. Jennifer reached the two.

Mary said, "Wet your skirt in a pool and wipe his face clean."

Jennifer hurried to do her bidding. Never had she seen Mary so tender. She cradled the man in her arms while Jennifer kneeled and cleansed his face. His eyes opened and he stared at Mary. He smiled as if he knew her. Jennifer said to herself, "He is handsome."

Then the young man started up. "Where am I?" he cried.

Mary and Jennifer helped him to stand. He looked wildly at the rocks and sea. Mary said simply, "We came to find you and now you must go home with us."

Jennifer supported him on one side, Mary on the other. "Where did you come from, sir?" Jennifer's voice was timid. There was something so spooky about the affair that she trembled with fear.

"I escaped . . . from the ship . . . I swam here." His words were broken and his eyes grew wild. He scanned the ocean for sight of a ship that would be looking for him.

Mary needed no more explanation. "Come with us," she repeated. "Come home with us and we will shelter you and hide you."

Jennifer saw the look he gave her. It was full of love and trust. Together they helped him to climb over the

boulders. By the time they reached the Witch House, he
was stumbling.

"Jen, get Grandpa," Mary urged. She could hardly
stand up, for the weight of the young man had grown heav-
ier as his strength failed.

Grandpa took one look at the young man and his uniform. Then he put his strong arms around him and half
carried him into the house. He knew that British uniform
and he was worried. In no time a hot toddy was prepared
and soon after Mrs. Rowe had a meal of beans and corn
bread ready. Grandpa urged him to eat and asked no questions, for the stranger was so limp and faint that Grandpa
had to half lug him up the steep stairs to William's room.
When Grandpa came down half an hour later he was very
sober.

"What's his name?" Cyrus pestered. "How long is he
going to stay?"

Grandpa put a hand on Cyrus's head. "Mind your
manners; be courteous to the stranger in the house. I don't
know the answer to your questions yet. He needs rest and
sleep and don't you go tooting your noisy horn or I'll spank
you." Grandpa scowled at Cyrus.

He went back up the stairs quietly and soon came
down with the wet and soggy uniform. He took it outdoors
to dry in the sun.

Jennifer spoke up. "If anybody should come here and
see a British uniform on the line, we might get into trouble. Let's hang it in the hayloft."

"You are a wise child, we'll do just that." He scrambled up the rickety ladder to the hayloft with Jennifer
right behind him. The air was sweet and dry as they rigged
up a couple of poles and spread the uniform across them to
dry. Then they went down the ladder and Grandpa told
Jennifer to warn the rest of the family not to say a word to
anybody about the young man now sleeping in William's
bed.

"This is our secret and until we know more about this young fellow we are not to speak of it. I am going down to your father's shop to tell him what happened today. Did you meet anyone on the way?"

"No, Grandpa." Jennifer was bothered as she said this. Was this not proof that Mary was a witch who knew about things before they happened? The way Mary and the young man had looked at each other made her feel sure that they were instantly in love. It was so eerie that she shivered with gooseflesh on her arms. She hurried into the house, glad to get back to duties which were the same as always.

· CHAPTER EIGHT ·

JENNIFER did not see the young man for several days because he developed a fever. She was given the task of preparing brewis, a dish good for the sick, made of crusts of bread soaked in hot milk with a bit of butter added.

Mrs. Rowe did all the nursing and not until the invalid was ready to come down stairs did Jennifer see him again. He was just as good-looking as she first thought, a slender young man with glowing dark eyes and dark wavy hair.

In the meantime Grandpa had learned that the stranger's name was Stephen Knutsford. He was the third son, not the heir, of Lord Knutsford whose estate was at Knutsford, or Canute's Ford, in Cheshire, England.

Grandpa told Jennifer how Stephen had joined the King's Navy and how later he came to despise it, because he had no heart for that kind of life, or for war. Stephen hated to see the American fishermen captured and forced to serve the king. He loathed to see the English sailors forage for food on American coasts. Often they shot the farmers who did not want to give up their cattle. Grandpa said indignantly, "He saw them shoot at a young girl who was herding her cattle. They spared no one."

When Stephen was able to be about, Jennifer was disappointed that he would not tell her anything about his past life in England. Instead, he talked of other subjects that did not interest her.

Mary, however, talked with him easily. Stephen would recite poems and wrote some which she treasured and refused to show to Jennifer. Mary was looking bright and happy. She flew about doing all she could to make Stephen feel at home in the Witch House.

Grandpa impressed the family that they were not to tell the neighbors that Stephen had been found because Mary had had a vision of him lying on the shore.

"You see," Grandpa tried to explain, "he is regarded as a traitor and outcast. The laws of England are very severe when it comes to punishing deserters. When people ask about him say only that he is a visitor. That is a lie, but a white lie, because it is told to save this young man from certain death."

"What about his uniform?" Jennifer asked. "People will ask questions if they see him wearing it."

Mrs. Rowe had an answer to that problem. "I can dye the breeches in the dye left from Uncle Thomas's breeches. He can wear William's old shirts and we'll manage somehow."

Jennifer's father watched with troubled eyes the growing closeness of his lovely daughter Mary and the stranger. Mary, at times, was dreamier than ever, but it was a different kind of dreaminess. Her thoughts were not far away; they were concerned only with Stephen's welfare. She sewed him a fine shirt and she made him a jacket of the same wool her mother used for Uncle Thomas' breeches.

Stephen slipped easily into the family life. Several times Jennifer heard her parents and Grandpa discuss in low voices the problem that troubled them. Then one evening Grandpa stood up and said firmly, "He comes from a good family and loves Mary. She loved him even before she found him on the rocks. Let us give in to their wish for an early marriage. They are old enough to know their own minds."

Soon the neighbors began to gossip about the stranger living with the Rowes in the Witch House. Carrie Babson met Jennifer on the road and she teased, "Your sister put a spell on that man and he can't get away from your house."

"That's not true!" Jennifer cried. "He doesn't want to go away."

Carrie's eyes were bright with curiosity. "Where is his home?" she demanded.

Jennifer did not know what to say. "I don't know," she mumbled. "Anyway it is none of your business!" Jennifer had a rare fit of temper and she burst out, "He is a gentleman and you are no lady, so there."

Carrie looked surprised to see Jennifer so angry. It made her think that perhaps Jennifer was trying to conceal something and Carrie was determined to find out what Jennifer's secret was.

Jennifer heard Carrie screech. "And your grandpa is a Tory."

"My grandpa is not a Tory." Jennifer glared at Carrie. She walked away but the troubled pounding of her heart did not stop until she reached her father's cooperage. Looking in the open door she watched him shape the slender branches of birch, hickory and ash. He bent them around the staves of the barrel until they held them tightly and securely.

After Mr. Rowe had finished with the barrel hoops he looked at Jennifer's face and said, "Is something troubling you, Jennie?"

He sat on a wooden bench and drew her down beside him. As he stroked her tumbled hair, she felt the strength of his body and his tenderness and it comforted her and quieted her angry thoughts. She took a slow breath and spoke. "I feel so good when I am with you, Father. I was mad because Carrie Babson tried to find out about Stephen."

"Well," her father began. "Carrie is like all the other people around here who are curious about Stephen. I suppose we would be curious too, if a neighbor suddenly had a stranger living with them."

Jennifer was resting quietly against her father when he gave her a squeeze and asked, "How big are the catnip plants now?"

Jennifer jumped up. "I think in a few days I will pick some and peddle them from house to house. Then I'll save my money for red leather dancing slippers."

"Jennie, save your money for something more reasonable. You like pretty things just as your mother does, I know. But you are too young for dancing slippers," her father said.

Before Jennifer could say more, he poked around in the open loft of the shop and brought down a basket. "Here is a basket for your catnip. Now run along and help your mother. I will be home in an hour and I want supper on the table because I am going to help a carpenter put a roof on the house he is building." Mr. Rowe turned the hour glass over so he could keep track of the time.

Jennifer walked slowly up the lane to the Witch House. She saw Mary and Stephen standing under the trees. Mary's head was bent down and Stephen appeared to be talking earnestly to her. Long rays of the sun shot through the grove and surrounded them in what seemed to be a haze of gold.

Jennifer knew that her parents had said they could be married in the late summer or early fall. She smiled to herself and went in to help with supper. Just as it was ready, her father came in and asked Cyrus to say grace. Then Grandpa began, "When I was a boy in London . . ."

Everybody ate steadily except Grandpa who loved to talk about his boyhood.

After supper Mr. Rowe hurried off to help with the roof while there was enough daylight. Jennifer cleaned and swept the hearth and put the dishes away. Mrs. Rowe sat in the garden with her sewing. Mary picked up a shirt to sew on and Stephen stood in the doorway, his eyes suddenly sad and lonely. Jennifer slipped up beside him, and asked, "Are you homesick, Stephen?"

For a moment he was silent. "I can't forget the high cliffs, the flying crests of waves and the spray blowing back like the manes of prancing white horses," he told her.

Jennifer had never heard anyone talk like that. His words made her feel as if she could see what he saw in his mind's eye.

He went on, "My sisters, one of them your age, and my mother and father and my two older brothers will always be dear to me."

"Do you want to go home to them?" Jennifer asked.

Stephen sighed. "I don't quite know." Then he said firmly, "Yes, I do know. I want to stay here. I can make a good life in this new country. I can be a teacher and have Mary for my wife. Some day when it is safe, I might take Mary for a visit there." He stared into the distance. Then he went on, almost talking to himself. "I would be a disgrace to my father. I went into the Navy only to please him. I wanted to be a poet because I love books and reading but that seemed silly to him."

Jennifer thought of the day Mary had found him on the rocks and she asked, "Do you mind if Mary is a witch?"

Stephen's eyes grew bright and his sadness was gone in a flash. "A witch? Mary isn't a witch; she is a lovely young woman with a rare gift. She sometimes has knowledge of things that are going to happen."

"I'm glad she dreamed about finding you on the rocks."

"Hummm," Stephen thought back to that day. "What has become of my uniform coat?"

Jennifer told him, "No one will ever discover it and find out that you are a British deserter. It has been tucked away in the bottom of a chest in the attic. There Mother smokes meat in the chimney and Grandpa hangs his braided strings of seed corn."

"Humm," Stephen murmured again. "I was worried someone might find it."

Jennifer chattered on. "Sometimes I put some of the shucked corn in the hot ashes in the fireplace and it pops and all the little white balls bounce into the room. I eat them and they are ever so good."

"How curious," Stephen said. "We don't have anything like that at Knutsford."

Jennifer saw that this was a good time to question him. "Did you live in a castle? Did you work in the fields and did you dig potatoes?"

Stephen laughed. "No, Jennifer, I don't know how to do any work. The castle had many people who worked, some in the stables, some in the kitchens and some keeping the rooms clean."

"My!" Jennifer was awed. "Wait till I tell Carrie Babson that you lived in a castle."

"No." Stephen's voice was stern. "You must not repeat anything I have told you. Promise me."

Jennifer soberly crossed her heart and promised not to tell a soul.

· CHAPTER NINE ·

ENNIFER'S basket was the subject of much talk. She
told the family she was going to pick bunches of catnip
and sell them. Cyrus begged to go with her but his mother
said he had to help Grandpa weed the potato patch.

Jennifer fixed herself a lunch, and set out for the catnip patch. She saw no one on the way except some of Babson's cows cropping grass in the distance and in a little while
she was busy picking catnip and tying the bunches with
long tough grass blades. The sun was warm and Jennifer
dreamed about dancing in red slippers. She could almost see
herself wearing a fine dress—as fine as any Carrie Babson
had.

When at last Jennifer sat down to eat her lunch, her
basket was more than half full of catnip. The strong smell
of the leaves was on her hands. They were stained, too, and
she rubbed them on her skirt. After she had finished eating,
she picked up the basket and started off on the road that
led all the way around Cape Ann. She began at the first
house. "Would you like to buy some fresh catnip, Ma'am?
Good for man or beast."

The housewife smiled. "How much is it?" she asked.

"A penny a bunch." Jennifer held up a bunch. It was sold.

She put the penny in her dress pocket and trotted along, going from house to house, finding customers who bought the catnip for tea which they said was good for fevers.

All afternoon Jennifer went from house to house until she was tired, thirsty and hot. She pushed back her sunbonnet and went to the kitchen door of a fine new house. Nobody answered her knock so she sat on a bench outside the house wishing for a drink of water. Around the corner of the house she could see the well. She pulled up the bucket and tipped the clumsy pail to her mouth and drank deeply while the water dribbled down her chin and the front of her dress. Satisfied at last, she drew her sleeve across her mouth and chin to dry them. Then she went to the bench to get her basket. The door opened suddenly and a boy stood staring at her in surpirse.

"Where did you come from?" he asked. "What are you doing here?"

Jennifer was embarrassed. She could only mumble, "I was thirsty."

"What is in your basket? Are you a peddler?" he asked.

"Yes," she murmured. "I am peddling catnip, good for men or beast."

"I never saw a girl peddler." The boy was curious. "What is your name and where do you live?"

Jennifer made a curtsy. "I am Jennifer Ann Rowe and I live not far from Haulabout Point."

The boy called into the house, "Sally, come here."

Jennifer looked up to see a girl, who seemed a bit older than herself and who wore her long straight hair caught back with a black velvet ribbon. Sally's blue dress was covered by a white pinafore with ruffles and a sash that tied in back. Jennifer had never seen any like it and she stared as if enchanted.

"This is Jennifer Ann Rowe, and this is my sister Sally Tarr," the boy said and both girls bobbed polite curtsys.

Jennifer turned to the boy. "What is your name?" she asked shyly.

"Henry Tarr," he told her.

Jennifer was delighted with their friendliness. She went with them into the house and they sat in the parlor and tried to talk like grownups until Henry suggested, "Let's not be so stiff. Let's play a game." He opened a box and tossed a set of dominoes on a table. Jennifer learned the game quickly. She forgot about her catnip business. After the game, she listened to Sally play on the spinet and she offered to sing, "Lavender's blue, dilly, dilly."

Then Jennifer invited Sally and Henry to play with her at the Witch House. She told them where it was and how it got its name.

"Is it cursed because it was a witch's house?" Sally asked.

Jennifer answered seriously. "I sometimes feel as if our house was blessing us and I think that some day I will discover what the blessing is."

Sally threw her arms around the younger girl. "I love you, Jennifer Ann," she cried impulsively.

Jennifer's face glowed with happiness. She felt as if she had found a friend. But when she picked up her basket of catnip, it was nearly empty. There were only two bunches left. She looked around the garden and saw three cats and a batch of half-grown kittens all rolling in the grass and kicking up their feet. They had stolen her catnip and were drunk with joy.

She had to laugh even if it meant the end of her peddling. She waved goodbye and turned toward home. To-morrow she would gather more catnip and travel further into Sandy Bay.

When Jennifer's mother heard about Sally and Henry Tarr she was delighted. "So that is who is living in the new house."

"I invited them to play with me and they are coming some day soon," Jennifer said.

Mrs. Rowe smiled. "How nice, you have had no visitors your own age. We must plan for them."

Mr. Rowe was interested in hearing how much money Jennifer had earned selling catnip. He was surprised that some people bought several bunches. When Jennifer counted her earnings, he said, "Fifty pennies! Put it away in a safe place and some day you will use it for . . ." She interrupted. "For dancing slippers."

Her father shook his head. "Don't get your heart set on something so frivolous, Jennie. You are still a little girl."

The next day was showery but between showers Jennifer gathered the rest of the catnip. She had to wait for a day that was fair before she hurried off again to Sandy Bay. She passed the house where Henry and Sally lived but saw no one about. She had good luck in Sandy Bay and when all the catnip was sold she got a ride home on a stone cart. The driver of the oxen was the same one she had met weeks ago. He chattered on about the young man who was living with the Rowe family.

"Where does he come from?" He pestered Jennifer with questions she found hard to answer without giving him information that her father and Grandpa had warned her not to give. Finally the driver jabbed his oxen angrily. "Is Mary in love with him? Aren't we Pigeon Covers good enough for her? She is stuck-up and she is a witch!"

Jennifer jumped off the stone cart, her nose in the air.

"Nobody can call my sister stuck-up or a witch!"

"Come back, Jennie, don't run away," he begged. "Come back."

Jennifer turned and made a face at him and stuck out her tongue. She yelled, "Boo! Boo!" and ran so fast with her clumsy basket that she tripped on a stone and came down flat on her face. She skinned her knees, tearing a hole right through her long skirts. Her chin was bruised and the palms of her hands were gritty with gravel and sand. Blood ran from her knees and she began to cry. As she sobbed and limped down the road toward the Witch House, a voice called after her, "Jennie, your basket and your pennies—you dropped them."

The driver ran to put the pennies in her hand and give her the basket. "I'm sorry I made you mad," he said.

Jennifer heard him hurry back to his team of oxen as she went down the path to the side door of the Witch House, calling, "Mary, Mary, come here!"

Mary took one look at her sister and at once sat her down in the house so she could wash her bleeding hands and knees. As she started to mend the torn dress, Jennifer blubbered, "He made me so mad, asking questions about Stephen and I lost some pennies, too."

Mary smiled. "But he found them and you have them safe, at least most of them. Now be a good girl and stop crying."

Jennifer was tired after her long day, but she stayed up to find out what her father and the carpenter, Mr. Hale, were talking about. Mr. Hale had come to look at a place in the woods where a small log house was to be built. It would have two rooms on each floor with fireplaces in each room from a large main chimney.

Who was going to live in the new house was no secret to Jennifer.

CHAPTER TEN

IT WAS fun to watch the building of the new house. Mr. Rowe gave Stephen and Mary the land for a wedding gift. Stephen learned to haul logs, from the woods, to trim and hold them in place. Jennifer ran to the carpenter's shop to bring him the tools he needed. She handed him the little wooden pegs that held the roof beams together and the floor boards down. The weather was good and the carpenter and his helpers worked from sunup to sundown.

The day came when the great chimney with its fireplaces was ready for the blessing. Stephen had learned about it from Jennifer. She began earnestly. "You see, if you place a dear treasure in a little corner among the stones, the house will be blessed. Have you a treasure, something hard to give up?"

Stephen regarded Jennifer's plain little face which glowed with an inner light. He was thoughtful for a few minutes. Slowly he drew a ring from his finger.

"My father gave it to me when I came of age, instead of giving it to my older brother who is the heir of Knutsford. Is this an American custom?" He smiled down at Jennifer. "I would give anything to bless the house where I will live in safety with Mary, my wife."

Jennifer took the ring in her hand and when Mary and the rest of the family arrived with a basket of lunch for the builders, Jennifer said, "Now the hollow is ready for your treasure. Have you brought it with you?"

Mary beamed. "I have the silver spoon Grandpa gave me when I was a baby. It is the only one left of all the family silver because the rest was sold to pay his passage to the colonies."

"Your silver spoon? Oh, Mary, how can you bear to give it up?"

Mary said, "I would give anything to bless the house where I will live with Stephen."

After lunch the treasures were sealed deep in a corner by more stones. The family watched closely. It was a solemn moment and Jennifer began to sing impulsively, "Praise God from Whom all blessings flow."

No one had planned to sing, but it seemed the natural thing to do and the ancient Doxology rang through the quiet woods.

Now the plaster was slapped between the stones and the chimney finished. When the setting sun showed the carpenters and the family that it was time to go to supper, everyone except Stephen and Mary left. They lingered to look at the little house from every angle before they could tear themselves away.

People were hearing about the new house and guessing that Mary and the stranger were going to be married and live in it. They had accepted the statement that Stephen was a friend who had decided to stay.

Mrs. Rowe had been spinning all year and saving up piles of wool yarn and linen thread. It was just about the time for the traveling weavers to arrive to weave it on the loom that stood in Grandpa's bedroom.

Grandpa was unhappy when they came for he could not lie down and take a snooze when he was sleepy. Nor could he use the bed at night. The pair of weavers took over his room entirely. He made himself a bed in the haymow.

Jennifer cooked extra food for the weavers. She flew around from early morning until the stars came out in the sky. A man on his way to Boston took Uncle Thomas's breeches and new shirts with him. He carried also a letter telling Uncle Thomas about Mary's wedding to Stephen Knutsford. But it said no more than that he was a well-educated gentleman who hoped to learn how to teach school. They asked for news of William from whom they had heard nothing, so far.

The day the weavers left, Jennifer was very busy cleaning Grandpa's room of lint and dust. She tied a cloth around her head and swept rolls of dust from under the bed. She shook the window curtains and so much dust flew from them, it made her sneeze. All the bedding had been taken out to air in the yard and when Jennie staggered in the door with it, Mary took one look at her.

"Jennie, don't do any more of that heavy work. Let Grandpa make up his bed, later."

Jennifer left the bundle on the ropes woven between the four sides of the bed. The mattress and sheet and blankets smelled fresh and clean.

"Where is Mother?" she asked.

"Resting on her bed," Mary said.

"Is she sick?" Jennifer questioned.

Mary held the big wooden spoon, suspended over the chowder kettle and turned to Jennifer. She said, "Mother is going to have a baby."

Jennifer was so surprised that she could not speak. "Baby?" she finally squeaked in a mousy little voice.

"Yes, Jennie, that is why she gets tired sometimes and needs to rest." Mary smiled. "Don't look so troubled, Jennie. Just think of a baby in the cradle and how you will rock him and sing lullabies to him and teach him to walk. Do you remember when Cyrus was born?"

Jennifer shook her head no. Then she smiled from ear to ear. "A baby to care for!" She hugged Mary. "I'm so happy and excited!"

Soon Jennifer went upstairs to see if her mother felt like coming down to dinner. Mrs. Rowe was sitting on the side of the bed, combing her hair, and twisting it into a knot on the back of her head. She smiled at Jennifer's big questioning eyes and said, "Somebody told you my secret."

Jennifer went to her mother and put her arms around her. "Mary told me that we are going to have a baby in the cradle. I will be glad to have a little sister to take care of."

"A sister? How do you know it won't be a brother?" her mother teased.

Jennifer said, "I guess I'd like a sister and I'll think of names for a girl."

They went downstairs for dinner. Stephen enjoyed haddock chowder. Mary was doing more cooking these days, getting ready to be a good wife and housekeeper.

The dishes had been washed and put away and the hearth swept clean when Jennifer heard a rapping at the front door, which was seldom used.

Mary said, "I'll go see who it is."

Stephen was still uneasy about strangers. Mrs. Rowe whispered, "Hide in the attic."

Jennifer began to tremble with suspense. Then Mary came back and beckoned her. "Some friends have come to pay you a visit."

Jennifer went to the best room and to her joy found the visitors to be Sally and Henry Tarr, all dressed up and acting very polite and grown up. Her pleasure made Jennifer forget how dusty her dress and shoes were and how snarled her hair was. She smiled happily at her guests. Sally began, "Our cousins the Rogers in Gloucester had a party and we met a girl who lives not far from here."

Jennifer's heart dropped. "Carrie Babson," she burst forth. "She had a new silk dress and dancing slippers."

Sally went on to tell Jennifer what fun she had at the party and what they had to eat. "We danced the minuet and the Virginia Reel. I just love dancing, don't you, Jennifer?"

Jennifer looked down at her feet in their homemade shoes. "I don't know how to dance," she admitted.

Henry laughed. "Don't look so gloomy, we'll teach you. Sally can play the minuet on the spinet and I'll be your partner and show you the steps. It is really quite simple."

"We don't have a spinet." Jennifer glanced around the room.

"Oh!" Sally giggled. "Henry means when you visit us. Will you come soon, Jennifer?"

Jennifer blushed with delight, and said, "Yes." Then she remembered her clumsy shoes. "I don't have dancing slippers," she added.

"No matter," Henry comforted her. "I don't have shoes made just for dancing, but I get along. I outgrew the slippers I had when we lived in Boston."

Sally teased, "Oh pooh, Henry you're too lazy to get new slippers and your shoes look so shabby because you climb trees to the tree house you and those boys are building."

Jennifer began to wonder what they could do to have fun.

"Would you like to see a real new house being built in the woods?" she asked.

They jumped up, eager to be outdoors, and followed Jennifer through the woods to a clearing where a charming little house stood. They stared at it and went inside where a carpenter was putting in windows with tiny diamond-shaped panes of glass. He told them the next step was to make inside blinds to close at night.

They climbed the narrow twisting stairway to look out the bedroom windows, right into the green hearts of the trees. Sally cried out, "Oh, I could be an enchanted princess living here waiting for a prince to find me and marry me!"

Jennifer was surprised. When she saw Henry regarding her with amusement, she blushed and felt so uncomfortable that she turned and ran down the steps and outdoors. In fact she was almost home before she remembered that she should be looking out for her visitors.

Sally flopped down on the bench built around the elm tree. She gasped, "My, you run faster than Henry!"

Jennifer was relieved when she saw Mary bringing them mugs of switchel and a plate of gingerbread.

After a pleasant chat with Mary, Sally and Henry got up to go home.

"Will you come to our house next week?" Sally asked. "We will teach you to dance."

Jennifer thanked her and said she would come next Tuesday afternoon if her mother did not need her. The children waved goodbye and Jennifer sat on the bench, thinking how wonderful it was to have friends.

• CHAPTER ELEVEN •

A FEW days later, Jennifer leaned over Mary's shoulder watching her write a list of furnishings she would need when she was married and lived in her own house.

"Four ladder-back chairs with rush seats and one trestle table, two stools and one four-posted bed with mattress and hangings. Two goose feather pillows." Mary read aloud as she wrote.

Jennifer said, "Mary, I want to give you a wedding gift."

Mary smiled. "Make me a broom of twigs."

"Oh," Jennifer cried. "I mean a gift that I can buy with some of the money from my catnip. What would it be, what would you like?"

She pressed against Mary in her eagerness and Mary laughed.

"Please tell me, Mary." Jennifer persisted.

"Well then," Mary began. "I would like an earthenware pudding pan. They had a few for sale in Sandy Bay but I don't know how much they cost."

The next day Jennifer asked permission to walk to

Sandy Bay, about a mile away. For some reason her feet felt
heavy and thick and she stopped when she came to the cobbler's shop for a short rest. "I wonder what red slippers
would cost," she said to herself. She was shy about entering
but after peering through the small-paned window she decided that the cobbler who had taken over Uncle Thomas's
business was a kindly man.

Jennifer stepped down into the shop and when the cobbler said, "Good morning," she dropped a curtsy and answered, "Good morning, sir."

She walked forward timidly and asked, "Do you make
red dancing slippers?"

"Yes, miss." He grinned. "Were you thinking about
ordering a pair for yourself?"

Jennifer nodded her head, yes. "But first I have to
know how much they would cost. I have some money saved
from selling catnip."

"Well now—" The cobbler was interested and asked
her name.

She told him she was Jennifer Ann Rowe, the cooper's
daughter.

He said, "And your sister is to wed and you need slippers to dance at the wedding?"

"O! no, sir, I don't know how to dance and the wedding will be very plain, the way Mary wants it," she explained earnestly. "You see, I might—I might learn to
dance. I—I might be invited to a party . . ." Her voice
trailed off into silence.

The cobbler murmured, "Humm-humm, well, I suppose such slippers would cost six or seven shillings. Your
feet are not very big. I will have to measure them."

Jennifer knew she did not have that amount and told
him she would come another time to be measured.

She left the shop and was coming near the general
store where housewares were sold when a sudden commo-

tion in the street brought the storekeeper and his clerks running outdoors.

A rider on a dusty horse shouted, "A battle has been fought on Bunker Hill, June 17! Many have been killed and wounded on both sides."

Jennifer cried out, "William Rowe, or Thomas Rowe, were they wounded?" She began to cry.

The rider had no names of the fighters. The storekeeper drew Jennifer into the shop and dried her tears on a red bandana handkerchief.

"What is your errand?" he asked, trying to divert her.

"I wanted to buy an earthenware pudding pan for my sister's wedding gift," she half sobbed.

"Look here," he coaxed her. "I have only a few pudding pans left and goodness knows when I will get more." He shook his head dolefully.

Tears spangled Jennifer's eyes but she looked at the two pudding pans. "How much does this one cost?" She pointed to one just right for a small family.

"Fifteen pennies and you are lucky to get it at that price," he said.

Jennifer's mind was in a whirl. If she bought the pudding pan it would be a long time before she earned enough money to order the red slippers. Soon however, she counted out her fifteen pennies.

And with the pan under her arm, she poked along the road home feeling tired and a little sad. But by the time she reached the Witch House, the air had freshened and Jennifer began to feel livelier. She flew into the kitchen, "Mary," she called. "There was a battle on Bunker Hill and maybe William and Uncle Thomas were in it. A man on horseback brought the news!"

"But he did not mention either, did he, Jen?" Mary asked.

"No," Jennifer admitted. Her heart grew lighter. She gave Mary the pudding pan and heard her exclaim that it was exactly what she wanted the most desirable and perfect pudding pan that anyone ever owned.

"Come on, Jennie, let's get dinner ready. Mother is sewing on my wedding dress. It needs a few changes because I am a bit smaller than Mother was when she wore the dress."

"I wish I had a new dress for the wedding," Jennifer said.

Mary turned away and Jennifer did not notice her sudden smile.

The prospect of her visit to Sally and Henry occupied all of Jennifer's thoughts the next few days. Tuesday afternoon she combed her hair neatly and put on a clean calico dress, but once at the Tarrs' house she had a fit of shyness. She was not used to visiting friends.

Hesitantly she lifted the brass knocker on the front door. When she heard someone coming, her heart beat too fast for comfort. Sally opened the door with chirping cries of welcome and led Jennifer into the parlor. Soon Sally's mother came into the room and Jennifer made her manners very correctly.

Mrs. Tarr was a bouncy plump woman who made a great fuss over Jennifer, saying how pleased she was to have Sally find a friend in Pigeon Cove. She left them just as Henry came. He greeted Jennifer with a wide smile and at once asked Sally to play a minuet.

Henry bowed before Jennifer, and she saw he had a scratch and a bump on his forehead. He took her hand and she followed his directions obediently, taking slow, measured steps back and forth, this way and that, as a delicate air tinkled from the spinet. As soon as she got the idea, Jennifer relaxed. She went through the stately dance figures with precision and delight. It was obvious that she was going to love dancing.

"You are a born dancer," Henry complimented her.

Sally turned and suggested they try a gavotte. "We learned it in dancing school," she told Jennifer.

"Dancing school? Is there a school to learn dancing?" Jennifer was astonished.

Sally told her that before moving to Pigeon Cove, they had lived in Boston. "That's where I learned to play the spinet, too," she said.

"Why did you come here to live?" Jennifer asked.

Henry explained that their father had been a merchant, importing foreign goods in his own ships from England, China, France and Germany. He had made money, but was losing his ships to pirates and to the British, so he decided to settle down in a quiet village and devote himself to writing a history of shipping.

Jennifer's eyes were round with amazement. She had never heard of anyone spending his life writing a book. In fact, she knew very little about books, except for the Bible and Dame Higgins' reader.

Sally said, "Father has a big room upstairs where he writes every day but, sometimes he takes us to Gloucester to visit our cousins the Rogers. We have fun playing in the ballroom. We'll take you there, some day," Sally said.

Jennifer could hardly believe her ears. Then Henry asked her to dance the minuet again. He decided that the gavotte was too complicated to try today. Jennifer was in a daze as she tried to pretend her clumsy shoes were light slippers and her dress was rustling thin silk. All too soon Mr. Tarr called them to take tea.

Henry refused to join in; he wanted to go out to his tree house. His mother said, "Do be careful, you are scratched already and have a swollen forehead from falling off a branch."

Henry gave Jennifer an impish wink and then he was gone.

China cups and saucers graced the table covered with a damask cloth. The tea service was silver. Pigeon Cove could never boast such grandeur. Jennifer drank her tea made from hot water, milk and sugar. No tea had been brought into New England since the famous Tea Party in Boston. She nibbled squares of crunchy short bread. She told Mrs. Tarr that her sister's wedding was to be when the house was ready, perhaps in late summer or early fall.

Sally interrupted, "She is going to live in the dearest little house you ever saw, in the woods, just like an enchanted princess in a fairy tale."

Then it was time for Jennifer to go home and Henry came running from the tree house. "Good-bye, Jennifer. Come again and we'll have more dancing lessons."

Jennifer smiled to herself all the way home because she had had such a good time learning to dance, and she was so happy to have friends.

• CHAPTER TWELVE •

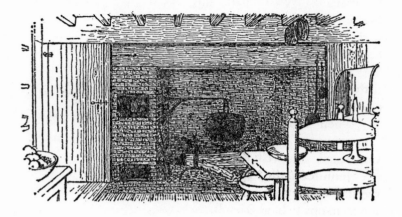

*T*HE summer days and weeks went by too fast, there was so much to be done before the wedding. Every member of the family helped. Mrs. Rowe spent many hours in her room, sewing furiously on the wedding garments and other things. No one was allowed to see what else she was working on.

At last the wedding day came at the beginning of September. Grandpa chopped off the heads of a number of chickens and Jennifer plucked the feathers to be saved for pillows. Mary baked bread, puddings and pies filled with apples and sweetened with molasses.

Mr. Rowe had finished the chairs and the table he had been making for Mary and he traded two fine barrels for a wedding cake made in Gloucester.

That Friday morning the sun rose on a perfect September day. Fresh clothes were laid out for the family. Jennifer helped to prepare a light lunch at noon but no one was hungry. They were too excited to eat when they thought of the feast to come. As soon as Jennifer washed and put away the dishes, she and Mary ran upstairs to dress.

Mrs. Rowe came in with the wedding dress. It was a heavy silk of blue and white stripes with tiny brown stripes between. She helped Mary slip it over her head and then Jennifer knelt on the floor and spread out the wide rustling skirt.

Mrs. Rowe smiled down at her. "Now it's your turn, Jennie."

She left the room and came back with a red linen frock trimmed with white ruffles around the low neck and at the edge of the short sleeves.

"For me?" Jennifer cried. "A new dress for me?" She could hardly wait to slip into it. Mary combed her hair for her and said, "Now let me tie it with the ribbon the peddler gave you."

Jennifer's eyes grew soft. "I remember that the peddler said I would wear it for a special occasion and this is it."

She stood at the blurry mirror looking at herself. Mrs. Rowe said, "Dear me, Jennifer, you are growing up. This dress makes you look quite a pretty young lady."

Cyrus was being stubborn until Grandpa took a firm hand and insisted that he have his face and hands scrubbed and his clothes changed.

Stephen had only the clothes he wore every day except for a fine new linen shirt Mary had made for him.

Finally the family gathered in the keeping room ready to start out through the woods for the church in Annisquam. Stephen had picked a bouquet of roses from the garden near the well for Mary to hold. The fragrance filled the room. Mr. Rowe picked roses for his wife to carry and a tiny bunch for Jennifer. The little procession started off with Stephen and Mary leading the way. Her parents followed, with Grandpa, Cyrus and Jennifer trailing after them.

When the processions came out of the woods into the open ground, the sexton saw them approaching. The wed-

ding bells began to peal a gay and happy sound, not like
the solemn Sunday bell.

The Reverend Ezra Leonard and his wife ascended
the church steps with dignity and gravity. A small gather-
ing of friends and neighbors of the Rowes entered next. As
the bridal couple slowly walked down the center aisle, the
bell stopped ringing.

Mary and Stephen came up to the parson and the cere-
mony began. Mr. Rowe gave his daughter in marriage.
Jennifer listened to the words the bride and groom repeated after the parson and she thought them beautiful.

Before anyone realized it, the time had come for Mary
and Stephen to sign the records of the Third Parish, Annisquam. Jennifer watched them and looked up to see someone standing at the church door, which was open, ready for
the departure of the wedding party. She felt her heart
turn over. It was William!

She ran to him crying out, "William, William!" and
flung herself into his arms.

The wedding party broke into a tumult of surprise
and happiness at the sight of William, in the flesh, with a
bandage around his head.

Mrs. Rowe's eyes filled with tears of happiness. Mr.
Rowe hugged his son and Cyrus clung to William's hand.
Grandpa seemed to swell with pride as he saw how solidly
William's frame had filled out and how sure of himself he
appeared.

"They made a man of you." Grandpa laid a hand on
William's shoulder. "Ay, you're a lad no longer and we're
glad Thomas got word to you."

Stephen and Mary had signed the register. Now they
turned to William. Stephen and William liked each other
at once. William shyly kissed the bride. The Rowes were
not much given to an outward show of their love and affec-
tion.

The wedding party went home along the wood's path, followed by the guests.

The merry din and clamor in the Witch House went on for hours. The roast chickens and all the other foods were eaten with mugs of switchel to wash them down. William ate until he could not cram down another chicken leg or slice of apple pie.

Mary cut her wedding cake and excited cries went up at the sight of the rich dark slices heavy with rare and expensive raisins, figs and dates. When the cake was nearly gone Mary asked Jennifer to save what was left. "You wrap it in letter paper and keep a small bit to put under your pillow to dream on. You'll dream of your future husband. Keep the larger piece for Stephen and me to eat when we have our first anniversary."

Jennifer was startled. She had not thought of being married nor of a lover, but she did as she was told. By the time she had finished wrapping the cake, Mary and Stephen had slipped away to their home in the woods. The neighbors were beginning to leave and Cyrus was sitting as close to William as he could, trying to keep his eyes open. Jennifer saw him yawn and then slump against William, fast asleep.

Grandpa was asking William all about his experiences. William explained that General George Washington had come to Boston in July. "I saw him as plain as I see you. I will follow the General to winter headquarters, I came home to tell you all good-bye, for I must go back in the morning."

It had been a joyful day but now it ended in tears. No one could persuade William to stay longer. He told the family how he had followed Uncle Thomas the night he ran away to Gloucester. "I believe with Uncle Thomas, that we enlisted in a glorious cause."

At last they went to bed. William had his old room

and Jennifer was alone in the big bed she had always shared with Mary. A piece of the wedding cake was under her pillow. It was a long time before she fell asleep. She missed the prayers she and Mary said together and the drowsy goodnights.

Jennifer did not dream of a future husband. She slept soundly until peal after peal of thunder shook the house. The rush and splash of rain brought her to her feet to shut the casement window. Thunder frightened her and she longed to have Mary there to comfort her. She crouched beneath the quilt, putting Mary's pillow over one ear and pressing the other into her own pillow.

She woke hearing her mother's voice. "Jennie, I declare, you have slept half the morning. Get up and after breakfast I want you to return all the borrowed mugs, plates and spoons to the neighbors."

As Jennifer put on a clean dress, she looked at the red frock hanging on a peg. Then she remembered something. "I want to say good-bye to William." Her mother's answer was sad. "He left very early and by this time he has met other soldiers in Gloucester who are marching to Boston."

Jennifer's lip trembled and she started to cry but her mother said, "William's choice is a noble one and he has given his promise to join General George Washington in winter headquarters."

Jennifer ate her breakfast and then filled a basket with the dishes to be returned. The mugs reminded her of the china cups and saucers the Tarrs used instead of pewter. She wondered when she would have a visit with them again. When the basket was emptied, Jennifer headed back toward the Witch House. Before she turned into the lane, she saw Carrie Babson and her young brothers tearing down the road yelling like Indians. The boys wore Indian head bands with turkey feathers.

They rushed up to Jennifer and clutched her wildly,

screeching, "Scalp her, scalp the girl from the Witch House!"

Jennifer swung her basket at them and kicked until the boys drew back. They had not expected such a show of spunk from Jennifer, who was usually rather meek and mild.

Carrie cried, "Let her alone, you are being very naughty!"

Jennie stopped fighting the boys and stared at Carrie with complete surprise. Carrie spoke stiffly. "My mother says she knows your folks. Besides, the Tarrs told her that they like you."

Carrie seemed embarrassed as she stood scuffing her shoes in the dust. "My mother says it is hard for us children to understand Mary and her dreams and visions, but she is not a witch." Carrie stared down at her feet.

Jennifer tried to speak but no words came. "Uh huh," she mumbled, and somehow that was enough.

Carrie called her brothers to go along home. She gave Jennifer what was meant to be a smile and then ran after the boys.

Jennifer's head was in a whirl. She hardly knew where she was going but her feet led her to the Witch House.

· CHAPTER THIRTEEN ·

*T*HE days of September were almost too short for all the work that had to be done. Grandpa was the one who looked after growing the supplies for the family. He had to see that there was enough to trade with other people who had goods to exchange. Grandpa cultivated the corn, potatoes, cabbages, onions and carrots while Jennifer and Cyrus pulled up hundreds of weeds. She grumbled about the work, for it was hard and made her feel cranky and cross.

After a long drink of water from the well, Jennifer sat on the bench around the elm tree and fanned her face with the bottom of her dress. She missed Mary since she had gone to live with Stephen in the new house. "I wonder what she is doing today—maybe she is baking a pudding in the pan I gave her." Jennifer sighed with heat and tiredness.

"Hi there!" she heard someone call. She turned to see Henry coming up the path, followed by Sally, pushing her hair back from her moist forehead.

"Hot today," Henry said.

Jennifer modestly dropped the hem of her skirt. Sally sat down beside her while Henry smiled at the girls.

Sally turned to Jennifer. "We came to ask if you can go to Gloucester tomorrow. We are visiting Uncle Daniel Rogers for the day, and he is taking us to see his vessels in the harbor."

Henry watched Jennifer with twinkling eyes. He always seemed to find something about her that amused him and it gave him a teasing expression. She felt shy. He said, "Will you go to Gloucester with us tomorrow, Jennifer?"

"I'll have to ask permission," Jennifer answered. "Will you come in the house with me?" She led them in the side door and found her mother sitting in a window with her sewing. Henry bowed and Sally curtsied and they began together, "May Jennifer . . ." Then they giggled. "You ask," Sally said. So Henry began again.

"May Jennifer spend the day with us in Gloucester tomorrow?"

Mrs. Rowe looked at Jennifer's pleading brown eyes and said, "If it is no trouble to you, she may go."

"Goody!" Sally jumped up and down and hugged Jennifer. "We'll stop by in the morning. My father is driving us."

Jennifer begged, "May I wear my new dress?"

Henry broke in, "Oh, wear an old dress because we are going to board some vessels and they are not very clean sometimes."

So it was settled. Sally and Henry went home and Jennifer dreamed of the sights she would see in Gloucester.

Jennifer was ready at nine o'clock when the Tarrs' carriage came rolling into the dooryard. Mr. Tarr stepped out and greeted Mrs. Rowe. Jennifer was amazed to see him so elegantly dressed. He wore a green velvet coat and a sprigged white vest with lace ruffles at his wrists and silver buckles on his shoes. Yet his manners were simple and he was cordial in his thanks to Mrs. Rowe for allowing her daughter to make it a pleasant excursion for Sally and Henry.

He helped Jennifer to step up and sit beside Sally, then climbed into the front seat with Henry. The horses turned out the lane and for the first time in her life, Jennifer was riding in a carriage.

The houses and farms and the shore went by like magic always bringing some new and fascinating scene into view. They drove past the Riverdale Mill where the miller ground corn into meal. Farms stretched along on one side of the road and on the other the ocean came into view and sparkled in the sunshine. In the distance was the town of Gloucester, where a forest of masts lifted against the sky and wooden wharves reached out into the harbor.

"Look!" Henry pointed. "Some of those ships are Uncle Daniel's."

Jennifer's eyes were dazzled with the sight. She had no idea so many people lived in Gloucester. Horses, oxen and wagons crowded the street and she wondered if Mr. Tarr could drive through safely. But he did, then turned the carriage away from the busy scene to where houses stood on higher lands. Their gardens reached down to the softly lapping harbor waters.

"This is Middle Street," Henry told her. He nudged Sally, who had fallen asleep in her corner of the carriage. "Sally! Wake up, you sleepy head."

Jennifer wondered how anyone could sleep when all these distracting and marvelous sights were there to be stared at. The horses swung into a drive and an old man with a wooden leg came to take them to the carriage house to feed and rest them.

After Mr. Tarr and Henry helped the girls down from the carriage, they went to a side door which was opened by a maid in apron and cap of frilled lawn, starched as stiff as wings. Jennifer was led by Sally into the back parlor to greet her aunt. Jennifer bobbed a curtsy and smiled shyly at Sally's Aunt Meg. She was impressed with the muslin and lace cap Aunt Meg wore and with her dress of lavender lawn sprigged with tiny pink roses.

Sally piped up, "Aunt Meg, we are going to show Jennifer the ships in the harbor. She has never seen one."

"Dear me," Aunt Meg sniffed as if she smelled something horrid. "Why do you want to show her those nasty, fishy-smelling boats?" She went on, "Wouldn't you rather sit in the garden and play quietly?"

"Oh pooh!" Henry cried. "Jennifer wouldn't mind a little fishy smell, would you, Jen?"

She flashed him a smile. She was aching for more adventures. Aunt Meg went on to ask if she knew the Babson children who lived in Pigeon Cove.

Jennifer admitted she knew Carrie. Aunt Meg said they were a fine family and Henry said Carrie was a great girl, full of fun and dash. Jennifer felt a prick of jealousy when he said that.

Then the maid came in to announce dinner. Uncle Daniel appeared in a plum colored broadcloth coat and wearing a powdered wig and silk stockings.

Dinner was not like any Jennifer had ever eaten before. A thin hot soup was followed by a bit of fried fish on her plate. Then a huge roast of beef was carved into thin pink slices with a red gravy flowing about them. Jennifer was used to well done meat.

The vegetables were plentiful and the raised rolls of white flour were tender and delicious. For dessert there was a baked custard.

Mr. Tarr and Uncle Daniel stayed at the table to sit over their port and crack walnuts. Sally, Jennifer and Henry went outdoors and raced down the terraces that led to the wharves.

Many vessels were tied there. Henry led the way to a large vessel and told the captain who they were and that they wished to come on board.

"Oh, indeed, Master Henry, you're welcome." The captain held out a hand to Sally and helped her up the gangplank. Jennifer climbed behind and Henry followed her. "I'll watch that you don't slip," he said.

Jennifer turned and gave him a snippy look. She could climb a gangplank with no help at all. She felt the deck sway under her feet with a motion that was delightful. Sally drew back her skirts when they went below, but Jennifer peered into every nook and cranny, exclaiming over the galley and bunks.

"Oh, I would love to sleep in a bunk and feel the waves rocking me all night long," she said.

Sally looked squeamish. "Ugh, I'd get seasick." She said.

"I see a bigger ship with taller masts, Henry. Could we go on board?" Jennifer cried. She felt bold in asking him but she wanted to be as gay and dashing as Carrie Babson. Something was driving her on.

Henry was amused at her enthusiasm and said, "Why not? That is Uncle Daniel's ship too. It sails to Bermuda and Jamaica to trade salt fish and bring back rum and molasses and other stuff. Come on, Sally."

Soon they were on board the brig *Nancy Lee,* and trotting around her decks. Jennifer was fascinated with the rigging, which a seaman was testing high up. She shaded her eyes with her hand and stared at him. "He can look over the town and the harbor and way out to sea," she said.

Suddenly, it seemed the most desirable thing to do— to climb the rigging. When the rigger came down, Jennifer strayed away from Sally and Henry who were chatting with the captain of the ship. She did not stop to think. She scrambled up and up the swaying ropes until she heard Sally's scream and Henry's panic-shaken cry, "Jennifer!"

Then the captain's voice, loud and forceful, shouted, "Come down, you little idiot!"

But Jennifer was too exhilarated and excited to heed

their warnings. For a few minutes she clung there looking over the town and the harbor and the rolling blue Atlantic. Then she started down, but it was so different from climbing up that her heart stuck in her throat and her feet froze to the rigging. She could not move.

This was not like climbing up and down the ladder to the hayloft at home. She was here forevermore, until she would fall from exhaustion into the dark murky waters lapping at the side of the ship. She shut her eyes and an awful sickness started in her stomach.

Faintly she heard Sally sobbing. Then she felt the rigging move and a firm hand was laid on her foot as a voice said, "Now, now, keep your head. Let one foot down and I'll place it on the ladder. Then the other . . . that's it."

Over and over Jennifer obeyed the calm voice. It seemed hours before she stood on the deck pale and shaken. The captain did not scold her. He only said, "You're nimble as a monkey."

"Oh, Jennifer," Sally wept. "I was so frightened for you." She hugged her friend.

Henry said, "That was higher than I'd ever dare to climb."

They went down the gangplank to the wharf. Henry cried, "Look, they have taken the bungs out of those barrels of molasses!"

Sally said, "Oh, what fun! Those boys are poking sticks in the bung holes and licking the molasses off. I want to try it."

The taste of molasses did not appeal to Jennifer for she was still squeamish. She watched Henry and Sally enjoy the molasses sticks until they were ready to go and climb the terraces to the Rogers house.

Mr. Tarr said, "Henry, you should have been here. We discussed the hard times that will come to the owners of fishing and trading vessels if this young revolution continues for any length of time."

Henry said, "Yes, Father," but without much enthusi-asm.

Mr. Tarr then called for the carriage and on the way home Henry pointed to a pair of stocks that had just been built for the punishment of lawbreakers. "Jen," he teased, "how would you like to be in the stocks with your head between those boards and your hands sticking out those two holes?"

She gave him a heart-broken look. She was sure he thought her a wild tomboy with no sense at all. She had tried to be bold and saucy like Carrie Babson because Henry liked Carrie's ways. She had failed.

• CHAPTER FOURTEEN •

JENNIFER was glad to see the witch house with its odd angles, and huge chimneys, standing among the elms and oaks. She thanked Sally and Henry and their father for a pleasant day, but when the carriage turned from the dooryard, she rushed into the keeping room and flung herself into her mother's arms with tears pouring down her face.

Mrs. Rowe said quietly, "What happened, Jennie?" She patted her daughter and soothed her until Jennifer could speak. "I'll never be invited again." She choked on a sob. "I behaved so badly."

Her father looked up from a chair seat he was mending. "I don't believe it, Jennie. Tell us what really happened."

Grandpa and Cyrus drew near. Grandpa had an amused look and Cyrus was all eyes and ears. Jennifer told them between noisy sobs just what she had done to show off in front of Henry. Grandpa chuckled, "You have all the spunk of the Rowe family, I declare—what a girl you are!"

Cyrus asked, "Were you scared?"

Jennifer told him, "I was too scared to come down and the captain had to help me."

Mrs. Rowe was serious. "There are pranks girls should not get into and this is one of them. Hereafter, remember that."

Jennifer did not want anything to eat for supper, so Mrs. Rowe took her upstairs to get ready for bed. She filled a bowl with water from a jug and told Jennifer to wash well. The bedclothes were turned back and Jennifer crept in. She was sure she had lost her precious new friends. She could not even say her prayers, she was so exhausted, and she slept at once.

Early the next morning Jennifer woke hearing the birds singing around the house. In the September heat she felt that the world was standing still and it cast an enchantment on her. Gone was the heart ache of yesterday. The fullness of the season was in the elm trees and oaks. The tangy smell of the sea stirred her blood and then she was wide awake.

Jennifer did not stop to dress but ran in her nightshift to the door and into the garden. She picked a bouquet and brought it in the house, tucking the stems into a jug. She stirred up the fire and hung a kettle of water fresh from the well. She tiptoed upstairs and dressed, rejoicing in the familiar routine of the day.

The family had not quite finished eating breakfast when Mary and Stephen came in, all smiles and eager to tell their good news. Stephen spoke first. "You will be glad to hear that I have been asked to take a course in teaching. The Reverend Mr. Leonard is making arrangements and he is going to sponsor me."

"When do you start to teach?" Mr. Rowe asked.

Jennifer could see how proud her father was to have a scholar in the family. Stephen said he didn't know. He was going to Boston with Ezra Leonard to buy some books.

"I told him about my background before he married

Mary and me and he feels sure I won't have any difficulty with those in authority for I have been well educated."

Mr. Rowe nodded. "That good man teaches school in Annisquam and I am glad to hear you two are friends."

Later the girls went to pick beachplums, filling the wooden buckets in a couple of hours. On the way home they made plans to go again in a few days.

"Of course, it all depends on when Mother has the new baby. Then you will be busy taking care of them," Mary said.

Jennifer's face showed her concern. "Will it be soon?" She went on, "What must I do? Tell me more."

Mary explained that when her mother had hard pains she would tell them to fetch the midwife, Marm Parsons. If their father was not in his cooperage, Jennifer would have to fetch Marm Parsons herself. "And you must have hot water on hand and don't worry if Mother cries with pain. She will forget her pains when she sees the new baby."

Jennifer tried to feel wise and ready for the arrival of the new baby but instead she felt rather shaky to have so much depend on her.

"Then when you have time, come and get me, even if it is at night." Mary told her. She turned into the path leading to her own home. They could hear Stephen chopping wood; the sound echoed through the woods. He was building up huge piles of logs because he would be too busy studying to chop wood for each day's use.

Two days later Mr. Rowe said he was going to Sandy Bay to have a talk with a man about mending his barrels. He said he couldn't tell the man how much work needed to be done until he actually saw the condition of the barrels. "I may go on board his vessel and sail around to Gloucester. This man has a brother who is in the market for a dozen new barrels. That means I won't be home until sometime the next day."

He looked at his wife and Jennifer saw his worried expression.

"Abby, do you feel well today?" he asked.

Mrs. Rowe laughed. "I feel wonderful. I could do a big wash today. In fact, this is a good wash day and that is just what I am going to do."

Jennifer enjoyed wash days. They came only once a month and everyone liked to see the flapping sheets, pillow cases and other linens drying in the breeze. Grandpa got out the big iron kettles and built a fire outdoors. Jennifer prodded and poked the wash with a long stick as it boiled and bubbled in the soapy water.

Mr. Rowe left on his trip. Cyrus and Grandpa went to the fields to weed and hoe. Jennifer and her mother bustled around. They sang,

"Oh, dear, what can the matter be, Johnny's so long at the Fair."

They sang all the verses. The day was perfect for washing and drying clothes. Late in the afternoon they folded the clean sheets and other linens and brought them in the house to store away in chests and drawers. Some things were set aside to be ironed the next day. It was early to bed that evening.

"Jennifer, wake up, child!" Jennifer did not want to wake up. She was having a happy dream all about dancing with Henry. It was a minuet and she was wearing red slippers.

"Jen, wake up!" She was being shaken.

"Humm?" she mumbled. Then she realized it was her mother's voice, sharp with urgency. She sat up. Her mother held a lighted candle, her hair hung down, and she said, "Get up and dress and run for Marm Parsons. Tell her to come at once!"

Jennifer saw her mother's lips press together to stifle a

cry. In no time Jennifer was dressed and running to the main road. There was enough moonlight for her to see the way and she knew it well. But the mystery of the night, with no one stirring, was awesome. In spite of the warmth of the air, Jennie shivered.

She banged on the door, and her voice crying, "Marm Parsons, come quick!" brought a figure in a voluminous nightshift and cap to the door. The woman held a flickering candle as she peered at Jennifer trembling with anxiety.

"I . . ." she could hardly speak. "I am Jennifer Rowe and my mother wants you at once." Her teeth chattered.

"Yes, yes, you go back and I'll be right along. I've got to dress and get my bag. See that there is hot water and don't worry."

The door closed and Jennifer ran home, her heart pounding so she could hardly breathe.

Once home Jennifer stirred the fire and filled a kettle with water. Then she went to her mother's room and saw her lying in bed, biting her lips and clenching her fists. Her face was wet with perspiration and Jennifer bathed her forehead with cool water.

Soon Marm Parsons came and sent Jennifer downstairs. "Stay there till I need you," she ordered.

Jennifer went down softly. There was no sound except for Grandpa's steady snoring behind his bedroom door. She sat on a stool, trying to get close to the warm hearth. She could not stop trembling.

Then she remembered Mary had asked her to come and get her, day or night. She rose and went out. The path to Mary's house was a new and rough one and the moon had gone behind a cloud. The woods were dark and still and an owl hooted, "Whooo, Whooo." A mouse skittered across her feet with a tiny squeak of terror.

Jennifer bumped into a tree and hurt her nose. She

put up her hand and it was wet with blood. She blundered into another tree and stumbled over its gnarled roots. Down she went, skinning her knees. She was so dazed that she lay there for a few minutes. Slowly she came to her senses and fumbled a more careful way to Mary's door.

She pounded on the door crying, "Mary, Mary!"

The door opened and Stephen stood there in his nightcap and nightshirt holding up a candle to see who was at the door.

"Jennie," he said. "What has happened? Your face is bloody!"

Mary rushed to the door. She took one look and said, "I'll be ready in a minute, Jennie, sit down and rest."

Stephen insisted on going with the sisters, carrying a lantern to light the path. As they entered the house, Grandpa was coming out of his room. "What's going on here?" he muttered and stifled a yawn.

Jennifer and Mary looked up the stairs. Marm Parsons was coming down carrying a little bundle in her arms and grinning from ear to ear.

"Got a little sister for you!" She sat down and opened the wrapping just enough for Jennifer to see a tiny screwed up red face and a bit of a mouth that opened to let out a brave cry.

Jennifer touched the soft cheek. "Nancy," she tried the name. "Nancy Lee." She held out her arms. "Let me hold her."

Marm Parsons laid the warm bundle in Jennifer's arms. The baby opened her eyes and they were the same misty blue as Mary's eyes.

Stephen and Mary hung over the baby and exchanged loving looks, and it was plain to see they wanted to have children to grow up in the new house.

Cyrus was scowling and pouting. He had sneaked down when he heard voices. "I don't want any more girls in the house. I want a brother. Take her away! I want a dog—I want a horse!" He leaned against Grandpa and bawled.

Marm Parsons took the baby away from Jennifer. She turned to face Grandpa and scolded, "Take that young one over your knee and spank him."

Grandpa chuckled. "His nose is out of joint, that's all. He's not our baby any longer." Cyrus was sent back to bed.

The sun came up and it was time to get breakfast. Mary and Stephen stayed to help Jennifer. After breakfast each took a turn going upstairs to see the mother of the new baby girl. Marm Parsons had the baby sleeping in the old cradle.

Jennifer came to the side of the bed and looked carefully at her mother's face. It was calm and relaxed. She smiled and said to Jennifer, "I hear you called the baby Nancy Lee. It is a nice name, but where did you get it?"

Jennifer leaned against the bed. "I saw that name on a vessel in Gloucester harbor and I liked it."

"I had thought the baby would be a boy and your father planned to name him John Henry for Grandpa. He also planned to name a girl Abigail, after me. You'll have to ask him about Nancy Lee."

Mrs. Rowe closed her eyes and sighed deeply. She was falling asleep. Jennifer tiptoed from the room. She made her bed and went to Cyrus's room at the back of house. He was sprawled across his bed and half the bedding was on the floor. His breathing was heavy. She looked at Cyrus closely and saw that his face was spotted with red dots.

She went downstairs and told Marm Parsons, "I think Cyrus is sick, his face is spotty."

The energetic Marm Parsons had finished her breakfast. She looked in her bag. "I got some camomile here and I'll brew him a drink. I thought that boy's tantrum was not natural. I'll bring down his fever and you keep him in bed and stay away from him in case it is catching. Your Grandpa can look after him."

Jennifer was relieved to have Marm Parsons take matters in her own hands. She felt tired and when Mary said she would stay all day to look after the cooking and cleaning, Jennifer asked, "Could I have a little nap?" She hardly heard Mary urge her to do just that, she was so eager to sleep after being up most of the night.

• CHAPTER FIFTEEN •

*W*HEN Mr. Rowe came home he found a jubilant family. Jennifer rushed to him crying, "Nancy Lee is here! She came last night!"

She hugged him and he looked at the others who were laughing at his bewilderment. Grandpa said, "Josiah, you have a new daughter."

"Is Abby all right?" Mr. Rowe darted for the stairway, not waiting for an answer and taking two steps at a time. Marm parsons left the parents and baby alone and came downstairs. She sat down with a groan. "I'm not as spry as I used to be." Then she turned to Grandpa and asked, "What did that boy have for supper yesterday?"

Grandpa told her, "We had boiled lobsters and that young one never wanted to eat them before, but he did yesterday. I took the meat out for him."

Marm Parsons nodded her head vigorously. "That boy's got a bad case of hives from eating lobsters. Some get hives from strawberries. I'll leave some herbs to steep in hot water and when the water is cool, bathe him with it several times a day. I gave him a physic a while ago. He'll itch like fury but in a day or two he'll be over it."

Jennifer was so happy that Cyrus didn't have anything contagious that she ran upstairs to sit with him and tell him stories. Her father came out of his bedroom wearing a broad smile.

"Well, Jennie, so you named the baby Nancy Lee from a ship in Gloucester. Why?"

Jennifer was thoughtful. "Well, I liked the name when I saw it and besides when I told Mary the name, she said it was suitable because the baby is going to go to far-away places when she is a grown lady."

"Mary!" He called down the stairs, "Come here."

Mary stood at the bottom of the stairs. He called down, "You have more notions in your head than a dog has fleas. But Nancy Lee is a pretty name and your mother likes it better than Abigail for the baby."

Mary looked startled, then she giggled a bit and said softly, "Nancy Lee is going to have a wonderful life, I know it."

Marm Parsons took her leave after Mr. Rowe had paid her for her services. She thanked him and told him that Jennifer was to come to her house the next day for a bundle of special herbs for Cyrus's hives.

Mary went home through the woods. Jennifer heard her father telling Grandpa how successful his business trip had been in Sandy Bay and Gloucester. "I'll need a horse to get around faster. This work will bring me enough money, with some barrels of my own, to swap for a horse."

He went on and on. Jennifer half listened; she was trying to remember the dream her mother had interrupted the night before. It was a lovely dream and she longed to get back to it, but she could not.

Grandpa stood up with a loud groan, complaining about his back because he had been hoeing all day. "It's nothing a good night's sleep won't cure." He chuckled and came to shake Jennifer's shoulder. "Did you tell your father how you got your scratched nose and skinned knees?"

Mr. Rowe had to hear all about Jennifer's wild journeys in the night to get Marm Parsons and to wake Mary. She leaned against him and felt his warm protective spirit comforting her. "My small brown bird, you are like your mother. I couldn't do without you."

Jennifer knew that she had a special place in his heart; neither Mary nor Nancy Lee could ever have the place meant only for her.

The next day Jennifer went to Marm Parsons to get the packet of herbs for Cyrus's hives. She knocked at the door and there was no answer. She stood patiently wondering what to do next. She was about to leave when a breathless girl came running up behind her. Jennifer turned to face Carrie Babson. But how different she seemed! Carrie was crying.

"Jennifer, my ma's going to have a baby and she wants Marm Parsons right away."

Jennifer's heart melted to see Carrie's distress. "I guess she isn't home," she said. "But don't worry, your mother will forget her pains when she sees the baby. I know, because we have a new baby sister born yesterday."

Carrie's eyes implored Jennifer to keep talking. "My mother is fine now and the baby's name is Nancy Lee. I named her for a ship I saw in Gloucester harbor."

Carrie grew calmer. Jennifer went on. "I was visiting the Rogers with Sally and Henry Tarr." Jennifer continued to describe the visit. She even told Carrie how naughty she had been.

By the time Marm Parson appeared from a neighboring house, Carrie had stopped weeping. Marm Parsons understood the situation in a jiffy and she said, "I'll get my bag, Carrie, and go right along to help your ma. But first I must get a packet of herbs for Cyrus Rowe." She went in the house and came out quickly, ordering Carrie to stay and visit with Jennifer. "I don't want you underfoot," she said.

They watched Marm Parsons with her wonderful bag,

trotting briskly toward the Babson Farm. The girls were suddenly tongue-tied and shy about being friendly. Carrie ended the silence. "Tell me more about that ship and how naughty you were and scared, too."

Now the ice was broken and they giggled and chattered until Jennifer remembered why she had come. "My stars!" she cried out just as Grandpa did. "I must hurry home with the herbs for Cyrus's itches!"

Carrie laughed and Jennifer told her how Cyrus ate lobsters for the first time and got spots all over him that itched like mad. "He can't ever eat lobster again," Jennifer said.

Carrie confided that she got hives if she ate too many strawberries.

"Would you like to see my new sister?" Jennifer asked.

Carrie nodded yes. They went off to the Witch House and Jennifer took Carrie upstairs. Mrs. Rowe was sitting up in bed, sewing. She welcomed Carrie and told her to look at Nancy Lee in the cradle.

"My! How tiny!" Carrie was surprised.

Jennifer asked her mother if she could get her anything and Mrs. Rowe said she would wait for dinner, which Mary was going to prepare.

"May Carrie stay for dinner?" Jennifer asked.

"Of course, unless her family will worry when she doesn't come home," Mrs. Rowe answered.

Carrie explained that her brothers had gone visiting relatives in Plum Cove. "I don't think anyone will miss me. The hired girl doesn't care who is there at mealtime."

Mrs. Rowe laid aside her sewing and Carrie asked if she was making a baby dress for Nancy Lee. "Yes," Mrs. Rowe said, "This is the christening dress. I'll sew a little cap for her too."

Jennifer cried out, "Why, that is the white stuff you bought from the peddler last spring!"

Her mother nodded. Mary came in with her mother's

dinner and her own. The girls went downstairs to eat theirs. Carrie enjoyed the fried halibut, and the tiny new potatoes and the squash from Grandpa's garden. Mary had sprinkled the vegetables with bits of mint leaves the way Stephen said it was done in England.

After dinner Carrie went home and Jennifer took up her usual duties. A few days later, when her mother sent her to Marm Parsons with a basket of eggs as a gift, Jennifer met Carrie on the road. Jennifer saw that she really wanted to be friendly. Carrie said, "My mother said I should ask you to come to our house. Would you come now?"

Jennifer smiled and nodded her desire to go for a visit at the Babson Farm. They walked along not saying a word.

This was Jennifer's first visit to such a big farm. There were several barns and outbuildings and a muddy yard filled with grunting pigs. The afternoon was almost over when Jennifer began to think of going home. But first they went into the house and the sound of a baby crying upstairs made Jennifer ask, "Did you get a little sister?"

Carrie said, "I got a sister *and* a brother."

"Twins! Jack and Jill!" Jennifer giggled.

Marm Parsons came down the stairs and said to Jennifer, "Come along now, I'm going to give you a packet of herbs to brew as a tonic for your mother."

The girls waved good-bye. Marm Parsons gave Jennifer the packet of herbs and instructions how to brew the tea. Then Jennifer was home again and busy as a bee getting supper ready. Her father came in and rushed to see his wife and new baby. Cyrus stood at the table when they were ready to eat and said grace. "Here a little child I stand . . ."

CHAPTER SIXTEEN

A *FEW* days later Jennifer's father came home riding on a horse. He had made a successful trade. The horse was young and frisky and Cyrus begged to be put up in the saddle at once. When he was up there, he looked down. Jennifer saw his surprise at how far away the solid ground appeared.

Jennifer asked, "What is the horse's name?"

"Major," her father told her. "You can fill that old bucket with water for him."

Jennifer took the wooden bucket to the well. It was fun to hear the horse drink and blow out his lips with a guzzling noise. Cyrus was so happy, he sniffed the animal and cried, "He smells horsey. I love Major."

Just before dinner time a rider came pounding down the lane with a letter from Uncle Thomas. The rider was invited to eat with them while Mr. Rowe read the letter aloud. In it Uncle Thomas complained, "We have a tough time of it. We are not allowed to leave the camp. We have not more than thirty-five men fit for duty."

He went on to grumble about picket duty, standing

still on a hill all night was hard work. "I was never used to such hardships before." Then he stated that he felt sure a major engagement was coming.

The family looked sober. There didn't seem to be anything glorious in this war. Uncle Thomas thanked him for his shirts and breeches and said he longed for a good bowl of succotash.

Grandpa remarked that Thomas was always a good eater. "I guess sitting on a cobbler's bench didn't fit him for picket duty."

Jennifer had not been listening with much interest until the mention of a cobbler's bench, but then she felt a great longing rise up in her for red slippers. But it was no use. She did not have enough money to have them made and there was no way to earn more.

After washing dishes and brushing the hearth, Jennifer carried the new butter to the cellar, making another trip to take a jug of buttermilk to be chilled in the damp hollow. There was a door built into the ground that led to the cellar. Here the fall apples would be stored in barrels. Potatoes and turnips were piled in bins, and carrots and onions were buried in sand to keep them firm until spring.

Mary was proud that her new house had a trap door in the kitchen floor. "I can climb down and get potatoes and turnips without going out doors," she bragged.

After dinner Jennifer found time to sit on the bench under the elm tree, swinging to and fro. She appeared very idle but her head was buzzing with ideas. Jennifer was remembering how nice it was that Carrie was beginning to be friendly with her. Also, she longed to see Sally and Henry Tarr. Then her mind got busy thinking about her new sister for she could hear the fretful cries of a hungry baby mingled with the soft sounds of mourning doves cooing near the barn.

The baby must be christened soon, Jennifer thought. She leaned back against the rough tree, on the edge of a drowsy afternoon nap. She slipped over the edge and a dream began.

She was dancing the minuet. She heard the tinkly sounds of a spinet and a voice whispering, "Jennifer, Jennifer . . . JENNIFER!"

This voice was no dream. She awoke with a start and there stood Henry, his teasing eyes twinkling. She sat up straight and stared at him, as Sally pushed him away. "We woke you," she said.

Jennifer was embarrassed to have Henry discover her napping. She jumped to her feet and Henry at once took her hand, bowed and whistled the tune of their minuet. Sally giggled. Jennifer felt clumsy, stepping this way and that on the tangled grass.

When Henry led her back to the bench and bowed low she gave him a broad smile. "I love dancing," she told him.

"Do you like dancing with me better than with anyone else?" he teased.

Jennifer said simply, "You are the only boy I ever danced with."

Sally poked Henry in the ribs. "Stop teasing and tell Jennie our news."

Henry said, "It's about my father. He is making a fuss about education. He says he would never have moved to such a backward place as Sandy Bay, if he'd known there was no proper school."

Jennifer was astonished. She had not known that people cared so much about schools. She did not. Arithmetic was horrible and spelling, worse.

Henry went on. "My father is going to look for an educated man in Sandy Bay to teach us."

Sally spoke up. "Our father has a good education because he lived in Boston."

Jennifer thought how dreadful it would be if the Tarrs left Sandy Bay because there was no good school. She had an idea.

"Your father ought to talk to Stephen. He is well educated and is studying now with the Reverend Ezra Leonard to learn how to teach school."

The visitors were impressed. At that moment Mrs. Rowe came out of the house and greeted Sally and Henry. Sally asked Mrs. Rowe about the baby and said Nancy Lee was a sweet name, but Henry broke into boisterous laughter. He glanced at Jennifer who grew flustered and red in the face. However, she calmed down when she saw that her mother enjoyed Sally and Henry. Jennifer told them the baby was to be christened the following Sunday in Annisquam, and her mother invited them to the feast afterward. The young Tarrs accepted the invitation with delight, and soon left with proper good-byes.

On Sunday morning the horse carried Jennifer's parents and the baby through the woods to church. When they arrived a number of people were putting on their shoes which they carried because shoes were valuable and had to be saved for church or other special occasions.

The bell was tolling with its usual Sunday solemnity as they entered. The baby in her white christening robe and tiny cap slept in her mother's arms during the service. Then came the time when the Reverend Ezra Leonard filled the silver christening bowl with water from a small silver ewer. He read the service and the baby's parents and godparents made their responses in hushed voices. Then the parson sprinkled water on the baby's head and named her Nancy Lee and made the sign of the cross on her forehead. She squirmed and cried, but everyone was used to babies crying when christened. The old timers said it meant that the Devil was going out of the baby when it cried loudly.

Once they were at home, Jennifer and Mary took over the cooking. A few friends and relatives who had been at church, sat under the trees. Indoors the fire burned steadily, heating the succotash made from corn cut from the cob and shell beans. It was served in bowls.

Henry and Sally came in time to feast with them. Jennifer wished William could have been there for this wonderful occasion. He loved succotash and melons warm with sun and sweet as sugar, but of course he did not even know he had a new sister.

The afternoon wore away. Henry took Cyrus for a row on the duck pond. The other guests went home to do their chores, but Sally and Henry lingered. They thought Cyrus a most engaging little boy and listened to his tales about what he was going to do when he was a man.

Just as suppertime drew near, Carrie Babson and her brothers came trotting down from the main road. Jennifer was pleased to see Carrie make her manners to Mary and the little brothers did the same. Henry and Sally hailed Carrie with cries of welcome. Jennifer felt a pang of jealousy when she saw Henry's warm pleasure in Carrie's company.

Cyrus took Carrie's brothers to see Major, the horse. They tore off with vigour, leaving Mrs. Rowe looking dismayed, there were so many more people for supper than she had counted on. Jennifer knew her mother would ask them to stay. It was the proper thing to do and no one was ever turned away hungry.

Mary ran to her house and came back with a basket of gingerbread. Grandpa brought in the milk and said he would fetch some eggs to fry, and some lettuce for a salad.

The youngsters gathered at the long trestle table on chairs, stools and benches. It was a jolly meal and Jennifer was completely happy.

CHAPTER SEVENTEEN

AFTER the christening Jennifer found herself longing more and more for red slippers. She asked her mother if she could be spared long enough to gather dry catnip.

Mrs. Rowe thought she was foolish to set her heart on the red slippers. "Besides, Jennie, where would you wear them? Remember you are still a little girl."

Jennifer smiled to herself. She had a strong feeling that she must carry out her plans to peddle catnip again. Going to the stretch of land near Haulabout Point was a pleasant walk and she was happy to find plenty of catnip strong and sturdy with flowering tops. She picked bunches of it and tied them with long blades of tough grass, singing to herself, "Lavender's blue, dilly, dilly."

Jennifer finally turned home with a full basket and the next day set out for Sandy Bay. At a corner she met a stone cart drawn by a team of oxen and asked the driver if she could beg a ride. He was glad to have company and chattered away to Jennifer. He told her, "Last night at the Punch Bowl Tavern I heard a fisherman bragging that he was going to get a reward if he could find a British deserter supposed to be somewhere on Cape Ann. The man slipped down a rope and swam off, they said."

Jennifer's face froze into a mask. She prickled all over with a sense of danger. "I guess that fisherman is a Tory. How did he find out about the deserter?" she asked.

The driver shook his head. "It seems he was out beyond the islands and a ship stopped and took his fish. He was too scared to object much. He told them he was a poor fisherman and no good as a sailor if they thought of pressing him into their service. He had a lame leg besides. That's when they offered him a reward if he could tell them the whereabouts of the British deserter."

Jennifer saw that they had reached the center of town and she hopped off and thanked him for the ride.

Jennifer knocked at door after door. "Catnip? Good for man or beast, a penny a bunch."

She had good sales on Main street and then she came to Dock Square and rested under the elm. She looked toward Bearskin Neck and saw the sign, PUNCH BOWL TAVERN, swinging in the breeze.

She was timid about entering such a place but something drove her on. She was going to do all in her power to find out more about the fisherman looking for Stephen Knutsford. She stepped into the tavern, a dark smelly room, deserted at this time of the day. A door opened at the far end and a fat woman with a bucket and scrubbing brush came in. She stared at Jennifer, a little girl in a brown dress with a huge basket of catnip. She was followed by a large yellow tom cat who ran to the basket with such excitement that the fat woman laughed heartily.

Jennifer spoke up. "Catnip, ma'am? Good for man or beast, a penny a bunch."

The woman opened a leather bag she kept behind the bar and gave Jennifer three pennies for three bunches of catnip. She had twinkly black eyes above a nubbin of a

nose and her chins and cheeks were like plump pincush-
ions.

"Come and sit down, little girl. You look hot and
tired. Would you like a drink?" Jennifer's look of horror
made the woman snort with amusement.

"I didn't mean a drink of grog, my lass, but some
switchel. I've seen witches from Dogtown Common selling
herbs, but this is the first time I've seen a child selling
them."

Jennifer put her basket on a table and the fat tavern
keeper chased her cat outdoors. "I can't trust that fellow
around all this catnip," she said. Then observing Jennifer's
curious looks around the tavern, she said, "I take it you've
never been in a tavern before. Well, it isn't open until later
in the day and then the fishermen come in to get their grog.
They don't have much money to spend with hard times
and the war and some fishermen are being stopped out
there." She pointed to the open sea.

"They have their catch taken by the British ships with
no pay and I bet some of them have been pressed into service by the British."

Jennifer was going to ask a question but the fat
woman continued, "There was that fisherman here last
night who had more money than the others. He was in his
cups and let on as how he was going to be rich as soon as he
found a British deserter who was hiding on Cape Ann. He
made a bargain with the officers who stole his fish right out
of the dory. But they gave him some money, saying he
would have more if he led them to the deserter."

Jennifer watched her pincushion cheeks and chins get
redder and redder with indignation.

"What is his name, ma'am? Does he live around here?"
Jennifer managed to break in. She was so scared that her
teeth started to chatter.

"Toby Poole, lately come from Essex. I hear. He's no

good, he's ready to betray anybody for money—he's a Tory and . . ."

Jennifer stood up. She stammered, "I must go ma'am." She hesitated and the woman supplied her name. "Ruggles, it is. And when you come this way again, be sure to stop. I use catnip for headaches." Jennifer hastily bobbed a curtsy and the door closed behind her. Gooseflesh crept up her arms and she shivered with fear. What could she do to save Stephen?

"I must tell Father right away," she decided. With her basket of catnip, not more than half sold, she put away all hopes for red slippers and half ran, half trotted until she came to the Tarrs' house. There she saw Mr. Tarr climbing into his carriage. When he turned the horses into the main road, she ran to him, crying out, "Mr. Tarr! Mr. Tarr!" If she could only get a ride to her father's cooperage!

As she caught up to the carriage, she dropped her basket accidentally. It rolled in front of the horses and frightened one of them. Mr. Tarr held the reins tight and controlled the horse. He saw Jennifer waving to him, but while she ran beside the carriage she stumbled and fell. He pulled up the horses in time to save her from being injured. He stared at her in complete surprise but not until she stood up did he recognize the frantic little figure, dusty and wild-looking.

"Oh, please," she wept, "let me ride with you."

"Jennifer Rowe, I declare, what is the matter?" he asked.

"I must hurry to tell my father something important!" she tried to explain. He did not know what to make of her anguished pleading but he said, "Climb up—I'm driving past his shop."

"What have you been doing in Sandy Bay?" he asked when they were going along.

Jennifer took a deep breath; she was calmer now and

she told him about her plan to sell catnip to earn enough money to buy red slippers. "For dancing," she added.

Mr. Tarr said, "My children love dancing. I wish they were more interested in learning. There isn't any school around here that I think much good. I hope you study hard, Jennifer."

She did not know what to say but she was spared further talk about schooling. The team stopped and Mr. Tarr said, "Here you are."

Jennifer scrambled out and dropped a curtsy. "Thank you, sir," she said.

The horses went off smartly and Jennifer burst into the cooperage. "Father! Father!" she cried. Her father looked up from his work. "What is it, Jennie?"

"Oh, father, I was in the Punch Bowl Tavern and I heard about Toby Poole, he is planning to turn Stephen over to the British."

She began to sob. Mr. Rowe took Jennifer's hand and led her to a bench. "I'm sorry you heard about that miserable business. I know all about it."

She looked at him, hardly understanding his words. "Tonight Toby Poole will be given a coat of tar and feathers and run out of town on a rail." He patted her shoulder.

"Will he be hurt?" Jennifer's tender heart could bear no violence to anyone.

Her father saw her concern. "Toby Poole won't be hurt, but he'll never forget that the American colonists are on guard every minute for traitors who conspire with the British." He was silent for a moment. Then he confessed. "Some friends of mine are vigilant, and we will take care of this business."

He held her close. "You are a patriot, Jennie. Now you run along home and don't go into the Punch Bowl Tavern again. In fact, don't go down Bearskin Neck, it's no place for a girl."

Jennifer felt comforted as she made her way home.

"Where have you been all this time?" her mother scolded.

Jennifer leaned against her mother who smelled of clean linen and not like the tavernkeeper with her sour disagreeable smell.

"Mother," she explained. "I picked all the catnip and I have only fourteen pennies and I lost some and broke my basket. I'll never have enough for red slippers." She buried her face in her mother's apron.

"I don't know why you have your heart so set on red slippers, Jennie. You will need some new plain shoes for school before long. I can see that you are outgrowing these and wearing holes in the soles."

Mrs. Rowe stood Jennifer off a bit and smiled at her. "Now you wash up and we'll have stewed blackberries and I think a Johnny cake baked on a board. It is time you learned to bake on a board so come downstairs in a few minutes."

Jennifer discovered that it was a very tricky dough to mix. "You see, Jennie, the dough must be just right so it doesn't run off the board when it is propped in front of the fire to bake," Mrs. Rowe said. Jennifer looked at the board, rather like a large shingle with edges that were charred from the heat of the fire. She was given a wooden spoon to stir the dough. "My, I'm a little scared to do this," she said.

"You'll learn how." Mrs. Rowe showed her the proper angle for the board and they watched the baking closely. Jennifer could not keep her eyes off the Johnny cake as it slowly changed from a slab of soft dough into a thick delicious cake. She was so proud that she demanded her father have the first piece. He smacked his lips and chuckled and said, "You're a good housekeeper, Jennie."

• CHAPTER EIGHTEEN •

AFTER that Jennifer was kept busy learning to sew.
She worked more willingly when she heard the soldiers looked like farmers because they had no uniforms.
The men who were called from the fields wore anything
handy, just as Uncle Thomas and William had. Their
clothes were soon in tatters and they wrote home asking for
more.

Mr. Rowe sent a letter to William telling about the
new baby and how Cyrus was jealous at first but now was
devoted to Nancy Lee. He told William that Stephen was
studying to teach school. He also wrote about the new
horse.

Sometimes Jennifer grew tired of sitting for hours
with a needle in her hand. She was glad when the bundle
went off to the soldiers. Each member of the family prayed
that the garments would reach their men safely. It often
happened that letters never reached their destination and
that could also be true of bundles of clothes.

Finally Jennifer had a change from sitting and sewing.
It was time to make apple butter. Grandpa built a fire out-

doors and filled a big kettle with windfalls. The finest apples in the orchard would be stored in barrels for the winter.

Stirring apple butter to keep it from scorching on the bottom of the kettle was a steady chore. Jennifer used a long smooth wooden paddle and when the molasses was added the bubbling mushy apples made the air smell wonderfully spicy.

The last days of October were so perfect and calm that Jennifer wished they would last forever and not bring her closer to the opening of school.

But they came to an end and when a storm swept up the coast with terrific winds, the people knew it was going to be a heavy blow. At first there was no rain. Then it began one night after the family had gone to bed. Thunder and lightning woke everyone—even Grandpa Rowe, who could usually sleep through any disturbance.

Jennifer got up to close her casement window. She tried to pull it shut but the wild wind pushed against it and she leaned out struggling with wet fingers to close it. The rain pelted down and in an instant her hair was soaked, rain poured down her face and all over her. It was cold and her nightshift stuck to her body.

The house's old timbers shook with the rolls of thunder. In a few moments, the lightning struck it and went down the chimney. Jennifer still hung out the window exhausted, with the wind pulling the casement away from her cold hands. Her feet were wet with the puddles she stood in.

"Father!" she screamed. Then the casement was torn from her hands with a crackling sound, and dropped to the ground. Lightning struck again with a great flash of light and Jennifer fell to the floor, moaning with fear and pain.

By this time everyone was up and hurrying about to see what damage had been done. When Mr. Rowe saw that only some stones had fallen away from the side of the chimney into the room, he said it was not important but could easily be repaired. There was no sign of fire from the lightning.

"Where is Jennie?" Mr. Rowe looked around at his sleepy family. Even Grandpa was there yawning and grumbling about being wakened. Mrs. Rowe held the baby, hushing her cries.

In an instant Mr. Rowe rushed to Jennifer's room. The rain was pouring in where the window had been torn off, while she lay crumpled in a corner, aware of nothing that was going on downstairs. She did not even know when her father burst into her room, gathered her into his arms, and laid her on the bed. She would learn later how he rode through the pelting rain to fetch the doctor.

In the meantime Cyrus looked out the window. "I see a big fire!" he cried in terror.

Grandpa peered through the wet window pane. "It's over toward the Babson Farm. Must have struck a barn— God pity the beasts if they didn't get out in time."

Cyrus sobbed, "Are horses beasts, Grandpa? Would God let horses be burned? I hate God!"

Grandpa took Cyrus on his knees. "Never say that again. I'll teach you a prayer I knew when I was a boy."

> *"From Ghoulies and ghosties*
> *and long leggety beasties,*
> *And things that go bump in the night,*
> *Good Lord, deliver us!"*

This was too much for Cyrus to figure out and he turned against Grandpa's comfortable chest and fell asleep.

At last the baby slept in her cradle. Mrs. Rowe started a fire. She cooked cornmeal mush and set the table for breakfast. She strained her ears to catch the sound of horse's hoofs in the dooryard.

Then she went up to take a look at Jennifer, but the girl did not stir. She was still unconscious. At last the door opened and Mr. Rowe and Dr. Jewett came in. The doctor took off his cape and tossed it over a chair near the fire. Rubbing his cold hands together, he ran upstairs with his black leather bag to look at Jennifer. Mr. Rowe went, too, but he asked his wife not to come.

Jennifer never knew how Dr. Jewett bent down to listen to her heart and breathing and to lift her eyelids and peer at her eyes. Her father thought he could not breathe, the suspense was terrible. The candle flickered and the doctor's shadow on the wall was huge and scary, until he stood up and spoke. "She has a concussion, I think, and there is nothing to be done but to let her lie there until she is conscious. Just keep her warm." He gave a few more instructions on how to care for her.

When Dr. Jewett left the Witch House, it was day and the storm had passed out to sea. Mary and Stephen came to see how much damage had been done. They had been snug and safe but the accident to Jennifer saddened them. Mr. Rowe brought the news that Dame Higgins's house had burned down but that the old lady was safe with her sister in Lanesville.

Mary said, "I wonder what Jennifer will say when she hears that a new school for children under twelve will have to be started—I know she didn't care much for Dame Higgins."

The next day Dr. Jewett came to look at Jennifer, but there was no change in her condition. That morning Cyrus slipped into Jennifer's room. He climbed up on her bed and patted her cheeks.

"Jennie, get up, come and play with me." He began to cry because she did not hear him. His sobs were so loud Mrs. Rowe flew up the stairs into the bedroom.

"Cyrus," she scolded, "don't touch Jennie. Get off that bed!"

Cyrus swallowed his sobs. "I only wanted to tell her that Babson's barn didn't burn—she would be glad to hear that the school burned down."

Mrs. Rowe gave him a spank and he went downstairs as fast as he could.

Late on the third day, Jennifer opened her eyes. She could see that it was bright daylight, but her legs were so weak that she could not get up. She sank back wondering what had happened.

Then her mother came in with Dr. Jewett, whom Jennifer had never seen before. "What happened?" she asked.

The doctor explained, "Jennifer, you were shocked by lightning and thrown across the room, banging your head on a bed post."

She put up her hands and felt the bandage on her head.

He said, "It is healing nicely and today you may sit up in bed and have food and drink. By tomorrow you will be out of bed and soon you'll be going to school." He patted her on the cheek.

"School?" Jennifer's voice faltered. She was not looking forward to school.

"Not Dame Higgins's school, her house was burned down but there'll be another school, don't worry, Jennifer," he told her.

Soon Jennifer was impatient to get out of bed and downstairs, for her strength came back quickly. The first thing she did was to inspect the side of the fireplace where a few stones had been knocked out by the lighting bolt. It was only a small opening, but she put in her hand and felt a loose stone—it moved.

"Father will have to fix this soon," she said to herself. "Maybe this hole is deeper than he thought." The stone was not large and it came out easily, but it left a hole in back of it. She put in her hand to pull away lumps of plaster but out came something that was not a lump of plaster. Jennifer looked and looked at a slender golden chain in her hand with a small dented locket dangling from it. It was dirty but unmistakable.

"MOTHER!" Come quick!" she cried with such an excited voice that Mrs. Rowe came flying from the best room, broom in hand, looking anxious and worried. She saw Jennifer's bright eyes and her face radiant with surprise and joy. "It is the treasure! It was put in the chimney corner by the people who built this house."

Mrs. Rowe gasped. "A gold chain! Is there anything else in there?" She reached in and pulled out a hunting knife, rusty with age, and an old piece of cloth that had once been a neckerchief but which now fell in shreds.

Jennifer's mind was in a whirl. These were the treasures the sons and their mother had given up in order to bless their house. It was just like Mary and Stephen who had sealed their treasures in a corner of their new chimney. Jennifer's pale face grew rosy and shone with pure happiness. "This isn't a Witch House! Mary isn't a witch!"

"She never was a witch," Mrs. Rowe declared.

Grandpa came in and beamed at Jennifer when she told him that this proved Mary was not a witch. He told Jennifer again that his own mother and sister, like Mary, often knew about things before they happened. "The vision Mary had of Stephen lying on the rocks, is called 'second-sight.' It was something she could see plainly in her mind's eye. People sometimes came to my mother for advice because of this. She was a very wise woman," Grandpa said. He went on to quote from the Bible that God moved in a mysterious way His wonders to perform.

It was not long before the news spread far and wide that the Witch House chimney had had a treasure hidden in it for more than eighty years. People nodded wisely and said they really had not believed that Mary Rowe was a witch. But as long as the house stood (which was for more than three hundred years), it was to be fondly called the Witch House.

CHAPTER NINETEEN

*T*HE family decided that the gold chain would be Jennifer's. Her twelfth birthday was in November and this was to be her birthday gift.

One day Carrie Babson came to bring Jennifer some black-eyed Susans from her garden and was surprised to find Jennifer quite well again with only a little scar to show where her head had been banged. Carrie saw the gold chain and the hollow where it had been found. She and Jennifer made up stories about the woman and her two sons from Salem who had come to Cape Ann to save her from being hanged on Gallows Hill.

Carrie whispered shyly that she was sorry she had been so mean to Jennifer at school. They wondered when the new school for older scholars, which they would attend, would be ready. Then Carrie told Jennifer that the Rogers family of Gloucester were going to have a dancing party and that she was invited to come with her parents.

Jennifer felt a familiar stab of jealousy as Carrie went on to say she supposed Henry and Sally Tarr would be there. "Henry is such a good dancer, I hope he asks me to dance with him."

"O, he will, I'm sure, and you will look so pretty in your silk dress and slippers, Carrie," Jennifer said. But every word was hard to speak, she wished so much it was about herself that she was talking.

Later that day Mrs. Rowe took Jennifer to the cobbler to order new shoes for school. The cobbler remembered Jennifer and he said the shoes would be ready in a week.

Jennifer's eyes strayed around the shop searching for a bit of red leather. She saw it hanging on a wall. "Look, Mother, see that red leather? I was saving my catnip money for slippers to be made from it."

The cobbler asked, "How much catnip did you sell?"

Jennifer told him about the first peddling trip and how much she earned but some of it, she told him, was spent to buy her sister a pudding pan. "I didn't sell much when I went out the last time, I had an accident and lost half of the bunches and some of my money."

"Umm, humm." The cobbler began tapping on his other work. He had his mouth full of little pegs, so he could not say any more and only nodded his head as if he understood what had happened.

Jennifer and her mother started towards home. They stopped at the cooperage and found Mr. Rowe ready to quit work and lock up the shop. He walked home with Jennifer on one side and his wife on the other, and Jennifer thought he had the look of a man content with his work and his family. She was happy feeling the strength and love of her parents.

To her joyful surprise, Jennifer had a visit from Henry and Sally Tarr a few days later. They brought her an invitation to the party at the Rogers' house. A few girls and boys were invited only because the day happened to be Henry's birthday. Sally told Jennifer, "We are to be there at five o'clock and you will drive with us in our carriage."

Jennifer's pleasure was plain to see. Henry said, "I

hope you will dance the minuet with me. You see there will be other boys who will ask you to dance."

"Oh, I love to dance with you, Henry. I don't want to dance with anyone else." Then she added, "But I must ask my mother if I may go with you."

Sally put her arm through Jennifer's, and Henry followed them to the little house in the woods. "My mother is helping Mary to pickle crabapples," Jennifer explained. Sally and Henry were delighted to see the new house now that it was being lived in. They admired the ladder-back chairs and the polished trestle table, the muslin curtains at the diamond-paned windows. Sally said, "How shiny your pewter is on the cupboard shelves—and the wooden bowls are pretty too."

The air was spicy and sharp with cinnamon and the scent of pickled crabapples. Mary was bustling around with such energy that no one would ever have thought she used to be sickly and dreamy and forgetful about her tasks.

They found Stephen reading and studying. He turned to Henry and said, "Can you recite your tables of weights and measures?" Stephen was trying out his ability to teach, Jennifer could see that.

Henry stuttered with surprise and Jennifer eyed him anxiously. She wanted him to be smart and know the answers. When he came to the end with, "Twelve sacks make a load, ten cowhides make one dicker," she was relieved, for Stephen said, "Correct." He was going to ask Sally a question, but Sally was wise enough to say, "Henry, we must be going home right away." They scampered off through the woods laughing and giggling because they had escaped further questions from Stephen.

Mrs. Rowe gave Jennifer permission to attend the party and Jennifer went home to get the noonday meal ready for Grandpa, Cyrus and her father. Her mother and the baby were spending the day with Mary.

After washing the dishes, Jennifer hurried up to her room. She looked at her red frock and caressed her gold chain and tiny locket. It seemed as if there should be something rare and precious in it, but she did not know what it would be. She held up the red velvet ribbon the peddler had given her and thought of his kindness to her. Then she looked at her badly worn shoes. At least her new school shoes would be ready for the party. Perhaps next summer she would peddle catnip again and earn enough for red slippers.

The day before the party, Jennifer's father brought home her new school shoes. He held something hidden behind his back.

"Which hand do you choose?" he teased.

She stood puzzled, eager to make the right choice.

"This one," she pointed. He held out an open hand.

"Oh," she was disappointed. "I choose the other hand!"

Mr. Rowe smiled at Jennie's long face. He held out the other hand to her. She stared and stared. "Red slippers!" Her voice came out in a high squeak. "Red slippers!" She threw her arms around him in an ecstasy of delight. "For me?"

"Who else? Who else is going to a fine dancing party in Gloucester but Mistress Jennifer Ann Rowe?"

It was a long time before the family could settle down. Mr. Rowe said the cobbler thought Jennifer a smart little girl to sell catnip to earn a pair of red slippers.

"Did you pay him for the slippers?" Jennifer asked.

"No, I paid him the money for your school shoes and I'll do some shingling for him. The slippers are a reward for your hard work selling catnip. You save your pennies for something else."

Jennifer hardly heard her father's words. She sat down and held the slippers to her cheek to feel their softness.

Then she slid her feet in and felt how flexible the soles were, perfect for dancing the minuet.

When the day came for Jennifer to put on her red frock and tie up her freshly washed hair with the red velvet ribbon, her mother fastened the gold chain around her neck and looked at her daughter. "Mind your manners," was all she said, but Jennifer could see that her mother was pleased with what she saw. Jennifer slipped into a fawn colored cape with a hood that Mary had worn when she was younger.

The Tarrs arrived right on time. Jennifer in all her glory sat in the back seat with Henry and Sally. The team of horses was full of ginger as they pranced over the road and it did not seem anytime before they turned into the Rogers' driveway.

The front door opened and the maid was there to show them where to lay off their bonnets and wraps. People came pouring in and Jennifer was bewildered by the sight of so much finery. There were gentlemen in powdered wigs and with silver buckles on their shoes. Ladies in silks and satins moved majestically. When she caught sight of Carrie Babson making her manners, Jennifer was glad to see someone she knew besides the Tarrs.

The ballroom on the third floor glittered with candle-light. A fiddler, a bassoon player and a man at the spinet, struck up a minuet. Henry, in very grown-up clothes, bowed before Jennifer. He took her hand and away they stepped.

"O," thought Jennifer, "How light my feet feel, how soft my red slippers are!" She wished the minuet would never end. But it did and Henry bowed again and then danced with Carrie Babson. Another boy was presented to Jennifer and she danced with him.

In about an hour, the company left the ballroom to go down the broad stairs to the dining room. Because it was wartime, the food was quite simple, but it was very good.

When the music began again, Henry danced with Jennifer. All too soon Mrs. Tarr told them to get ready to go home. Carrie's father called her and they all went out to their carriages.

From down the street came the voice of the town crier; "Ten o'clock and all's well . . . ten o'clock and all's well. . . ."

The only person awake on the drive home was Mr. Tarr. Sally leaned against Henry on one side and Jennifer leaned on the other side. He was cosy and soon felt sleepy too. His head bobbed up and down with the jolting of the wheels on the rough roads, but he did not wake.

In the dooryard of the Witch House, Mr. Rowe held up a lantern. He thanked Mr. and Mrs. Tarr and the young Tarrs for taking Jennifer to her first dancing party. Jennifer woke up in time to make her manners properly but her voice was sleepy. Sally and Henry roused themselves enough to call good-night.

Jennifer stretched and yawned. Her father looked at her red frock, red slippers and red hair ribbon. "Where is my little brown bird?" he teased. Jennifer laid her head against his warm firm body. All she could do was to giggle, "Oh Father!"

It was the middle of November before the new school was ready for pupils twelve years and older. The first day found Jennifer so early that she sat on the school steps waiting. This was an important day, for Stephen was about to start teaching in the new school. Henry and Sally joined her. Henry leaned down and picked a four-leaf clover.

"It means good luck," Sally said.

Henry gave it to Jennifer. "It's for you."

She beamed with bashful pleasure. "I'll put it in my locket and keep it forever," she said.

Stephen Knutsford arrived and went in, coming back

with a hand bell. He clanged it vigorously, summoning pupils to their seats on the long wooden benches. As she faced their new teacher, Jennifer saw that he had a friendly expression and thought to herself, "Maybe I will like school with Stephen for my teacher."

She stole a look along the row of boys and girls, neat and quiet and ready to be educated. Mostly she saw Carrie and Henry and Sally Tarr, her *very own friends*. For the first time in her life, Jennifer was almost sure that she was going to enjoy being in school.

DATE DUE

MAY 1 2 1972			
APR 19 '74			
APR 1 1974			
JUL 26 '74			
JUL 1 2 1974			
JUN 3 0 1975			
FEB 2 9 '80			
AUG 2 3 1985			
NOV 0 3 1991	NOV 0 7 1991		
	WITHDRAWN FROM		
	OHIO NORTHERN		
	UNIVERSITY LIBRARY		
GAYLORD			PRINTED IN U.S A.

HETERICK MEMORIAL LIBRARY
JF H723g   onujf
Holberg, Ruth Langl / The girl in the witc

3 5111 00157 1482